Split
Just
Right

Adele Griffin

Hyperion Books for Children
New York

Special thanks to Donna Bray,
my wise and tireless editor

First Edition
1 3 5 7 9 10 8 6 4 2

Printed in the United States of America.

This book is set in 12.5-point Berkeley Book.

Library of Congress Cataloging-in-Publication Data
Griffin, Adele.
Split just right / by Adele Griffin.
p.   cm.
Summary: After living her life in her actress mother's world of make-believe, ninth-grader Dandelion comes to realize that it is better to face reality.
ISBN 0-7868-0347-9 (trade)—ISBN 0-7868-2288-0 (lib. bdg.)
[1. Mothers and daughters—Fiction. 2. Single-parent family—Fiction.
3. Theater—Fiction.] I. Title.
PZ7.G881325Sp   1997
[Fic]—DC21   96-45403

For my mother

CHAPTER

1

"WA-WA."

That's the only word Helen Keller has to say in this play the Bellmont Players performed three years ago. One line, at the very end of the play, right after Helen's teacher, Annie Sullivan, spells the word *water* into Helen's hand. Helen, who's blind and deaf, is supposed to get an excited gleam in her unseeing eyes, because finally she understands there's a name for this wet stuff. The stage directions read: *"Helen falls to knees facing audience, splashes water from pump."*

"Wa-wa!" Helen says in a voice that Louis, the director, said should be something between a grunt and a mutter. "After all," Louis explained, "she can't exactly hear herself saying it, right?" Right. *Fade-out.* The lights dim as the crowd begins its thunderous applause, satisfied by the well-known and emotional ending of a well-known and emotional play. *Curtain.*

So, one word. Easy enough. Unless anyone was hoping for thunderous applause. Here's what the reviews said:

The Philadelphia Éclat:
As Helen Keller, Danny Finzimer gives a shockingly wooden performance that left this reviewer uncertain whether to laugh or scream.

The St. Germaine Weekly:
Finally, in one of the most difficult roles ever given to a child actor, Danny Finzimer's Helen lacks not only zim but also zam, zip, and any emotion in between.

The Suburban Review:
No word could accurately describe the pain of watching Danny Finzimer struggle with a role that, right from her opening scene, dangled entirely out of her grasp.

"Well, I myself am no stranger to the occasional bad review." Mom shrugged. "What doesn't kill you makes you stronger, right?"

Here's what the *Éclat* said about Annie Sullivan:

Is there any greater joy this season than to watch Susan Finzimer's portrayal of that feisty Irishwoman, Miss Sullivan? She captures all the dignity and spirit of the role, while at the same time infusing it with her own sanguine vulnerability.

There were plenty more good Susan Finzimer reviews, but I think just one makes the point clear. What none of the papers mentioned was that Danny Finzimer's bad reviews were all because Susan Finzimer could not afford a five-night-a-week baby-sitter.

"But I'm not a Bellmont Player," I told Mom right at the beginning. "I don't know how to be Helen Keller. I don't know how to be anything except me." Even at age eleven, I knew my limitations. Mom rolled her eyes up to the ceiling for answers.

"Look," she said. "I've already been cast as Annie. That's a huge role and I'm going to be in rehearsal all the time. I can't just leave you alone in the apartment night after night. Louis said you're good as cast if you try out. Come on, Danny, it'll be fun."

While I didn't die from bad reviews, I doubt they made me any stronger. In fact, the only thing they did make me was thankful that anyone who really was blind and deaf would never be in the audience to see and hear the disaster of me being Helen Keller. Another unfortunate side effect of the play was that Mom got this crazy idea in her head that, bad reviews or not, our being in a show together was a positive mother-daughter experience, meriting an encore performance.

I've tried talking sense into her. "It's good enough for me when you go to my basketball games, Mom," I explained. "I like knowing you're in the bleachers, but I never want to pass you the ball."

"But *As You Like It* is a comedy, with singing. And that's a whole different ball game, right? Plus you have such a beautiful voice, such great comic timing."

Although Mom persists, I haven't given in. When I come home from basketball practice this afternoon, I'm not even too surprised by the note folded up against half a head of lettuce in the refrigerator.

> Danny,
> There's bagels in the freezer to defrost for PB&J. I'll be back late. Louis said we need some more walk-ons for the wedding song, if you want to drop by and lend a voice. Get Gary to drive you—he already said he would. I'd love it if you came!
>
> Love, Mom

I toss the note in the trash and open the freezer.

"Knock knock." Gary's frizzy hair and one of his brown eyes appear from behind the apartment's front door. "You need a lift anywhere, like maybe the Bellmont People's Theater?"

"Very funny; I'm ignoring you. You want peanut

butter and jelly on freezer-burned bagels?"

"Again? No, no thanks. Anyway, I *told* Susan you'd never want to, but you know what they say: hope springs maternal. How about pizza?" Gary picks up the wall phone. "My treat."

I shove the bagels back inside their low-ceilinged igloo of our almost never defrosted freezer.

"With pepperoni?"

"Half nitrites for you, half green pepper for me. Okay?" I nod; he's already speaking to the pizza guy.

Gary lives in our apartment building, in 4B (Mom and I live in 4M). He's an analyst for a computer software company, which in my mind conjures up a blurry image of Gary sitting in a windowless gray room full of computers. The great thing about his job, though, is that for every birthday Gary gives me an amazing top-of-the-line computer appliance. Last year it was a color printer; the year before, a laptop. My room looks like I'm some kind of gadget geek, which is pretty ironic since I've mastered only the basic word-processing programs.

"One pizza for two is on its way," Gary says as he hangs up. "You better eat a few of my green peppers, though, so you at least can pretend to be getting some vegetables inside you."

"Sure," I lie. Cooked green peppers taste like bad breath. But Gary thinks all people's health and emotional problems lead back to their not getting enough vitamins or exercise.

"And are you still on to do the AIDS walkathon next weekend? Did you find a sponsor?"

"My coach, Mrs. Sherman, said she would."

"Nice work, Wombat." Gary grabs my nose, pinching it between his knuckles.

The years I've known Gary, which is pretty much my entire life, can be traced through the history of his nicknames for me. He started out calling me Dandelion (my real name), which he shortened to D. L., which turned into Deal, then Deal-a-Meal, which became Mealie, Mealie-worm, and then for a long time Worm until about a year ago, when he settled in on Wombat. It's an annoying name, but I guess Wombat beats Mealie-worm.

Mom sometimes calls Gary my second mother, since he's constantly on my back about doing homework and not eating fried honey-and-banana sandwiches for dinner (one of Mom's specialties). When I was younger, I used to wish that Mom and Gary would get married, but that was before I completely understood about

Elliot, Gary's boyfriend, who died of AIDS last spring. Elliot never would have let us order out for pizza; he would have invited me over to 4B for spaghetti with tofu meatballs and pretended to be mad when I fed a couple to Friday, their eternally hungry Labrador. I still really miss Elliot, and I know Gary does, too, even though he hardly ever talks about him.

"Hey, she's on in two minutes." Gary checks his sports watch. "Five twenty-eight, right? Before the local news. Where's your remote?" I buzz around the living room until I find it on top of the TV. Channel three is still running the credits on *Laverne and Shirley*. I flop in front of the set and open my math book. Gary sits down next to me.

"So, she told you, right?"

"Told me what?" I look up from the book.

"That she lost the deal? That they didn't—wait, turn it up." He presses the remote and the red thermometer of the volume bar inches upward. I stare at the screen, now starring Mom, who stands in the middle of a phony TV kitchen much bigger and way more expensive-looking than our tiny although hardly ever used one.

"My husband, Ned." She sighs and rolls her eyes at the sound of a deafening offscreen crash. "You can always depend on him to break anything he tries to fix. Which is why I always shop at Kahani's." The screen flashes to a split-screen shot of all three Kahani's appliance stores. Mom's voice-over rings tunefully, "Right off Route 29 in Kingston, the Kingston Plaza, or the Bide Away Shopping Mall, all Kahani stores have brand-name items, full-service warranties, and unbeatable everyday low prices. And Kahani's will match the lowest prices of any other store. That's right, any other price at any other store. Just bring in your receipt."

The screen switches back to Mom in her fake kitchen. A little girl, much younger and cuter than I am, runs in holding a sudsy shirt. Soap bubbles are blowing everywhere.

"Mommy, Mommy, Daddy tried to fix the washer," the girl squeals. Mom laughs and takes the shirt. "Don't worry, honey. There's always a Kahani's location nearby." Then, the same shot of Kahani's, this time with the phone numbers and addresses flashing below it in yellow type.

"Mom says that kid who plays her daughter has major halitosis."

"Hand it to Susan, though. Only she could make the happy homemaker look like a stellar career move."

Gary yawns and stretches his arms over his head. "She at rehearsal?"

"Yep, a late one. But what were you saying before, Gary? About losing a deal?"

"I feel very spill-the-beans-ish if you don't know." Gary squeezes the tip of his earlobe, a nervous habit he swears he doesn't have. "But the whole Kahani's chain is going bottom-up. With everyone buying from Value Center these days, Mr. and Mrs. Kahani decided to sell the business and spend their millions in a retirement resort in New Mexico. Which is great for them but bad for Susan, since that means they're not renewing her contract."

"Oh, wow." I close my math book and set it on the coffee table. "Even the New Jersey and Delaware stores?"

"Everything."

"She told you that? She told you and not me?" Gary nods. He looks uncomfortable. "Wow. When'd you find all this out?"

"Couple of days ago. Don't say I said anything, Wombat."

"No, I wouldn't." The news really shakes me up, though. I can't stop thinking about it, even after Gary leaves.

Mom has been Ned's Wife for as long as we've lived

in Foxwood, which is over eleven years—ever since we moved out of Philadelphia. The running joke of the ads is how you never see Ned—he's always off camera, making crashing, klutzy sounds. Mom's the star of all the Kahani's commercials, which makes her sort of a local celebrity; her picture is even up at the Laundromat. But more important than that, the Kahani's money provides a sizable chunk of our budget. Mom also teaches middle and upper school chorus, plus upper school drama club on Wednesdays and Fridays at my school, as well as being the box-office manager for the Bellmont People's Theater. She *is* one of the Bellmont Players, too, although unfortunately acting in a Bellmont production is nonpaying. Mostly, it's all the Kahani's ads that pay our rent.

Cleaning for diversion is not a trait I inherited from Mom, so there's plenty to keep me busy. I straighten and stack and even sweep a hand vacuum over the living-room curtains, which have collected a furry coat of dust. Mom's taste in decorating runs to buying yards of fabric, then draping it over all the walls, windows, and furniture. She picks only shades of off-white, too—colors like eggshell and buttermilk and vanilla. There's so much pale fabric draped and swathed through our apartment that Gary says it looks like a bridal shop.

After vacuuming the fabric, I use a ripped pillowcase to dust the bookshelf crowded mostly with pictures of me. A faded snapshot of Rick Finzimer, my dad, grins at me from its frame. In the picture, he's rock climbing and the background shows a mist of clouds edging the soft tips of a mountain range. When I was little I thought he was in heaven. Now I know he was only in Tibet, during the summer of his junior year in high school, so in the photo he's just a couple years older than I am now. His unworried smile is the one and only expression of his I know. I dust him off, too.

"You can clean but you can't hide," I imagine him saying through his white teeth. "What's going to happen without the Kahani's money? What are you and Mom going to do?" I frown at his smile and work my way back to the kitchen, then my room, then Mom's, where I attempt a search for the carpet, buried under piles of laundry, magazines, and crumpled Kleenexes.

The whole time I'm cleaning, I'm mentally riffling through the week, searching for clues about the Kahani's contract. Mom has been preoccupied, definitely, but I figured it was mostly due to the *As You Like It*

last-minute switch. She'd been depressed about being
Celia.

"Celia's so plain pudding," Mom complained whenever she and I ran lines. "How can Louis do this to me?"
Louis adores Mom, though, and so last Friday he
switched the Rosalind and Celia roles, and supposedly
Laura Drinker, the old Rosalind, pitched a big temper
tantrum and threw a stack of light gels right at the back
of Louis's bald head.

The last stop is the bathroom. As I'm scrubbing the
sink I look up and catch my reflection in the mirror.

"Oh, terrific." Little aspirin-sized red blotches are
spattered over my chest and neck. Gross-looking but
harmless, they appear whenever I'm anxious about
something. The first time I got them was in kindergarten. Mom rushed me to the doctor. After three very
different but all embarrassing tests, Dr. Gavin finally
pulled out the problem I'd been holding inside: that
earlier in the day I'd fed our class rabbit, Trouble, some
fingerpaints and was scared he was going to die.

The whole apartment is pin straight by the time the
eleven o'clock news airs. I've even polished every piece
of the glass collection we inherited in bulk after Mom
played Laura in *The Glass Menagerie*.

I sit tiredly in front of the TV, as Hal "Troubleshooter" Drummond explains how he and his news crew have discovered that some local movie theaters are storing popcorn in mouse-infested closets before putting it in those glass display cases. I close my eyes and try to recall any type of mouse taste from the last time Portia and I got popcorn at the movies. It's hard to remember, and I feel my bones starting to soften in their sockets, promising sleep.

"Danny?"

I jump, knocking my math book off my lap. Mom stands over me. Her overcoat smells like cigarettes and wet leaves. "You must have fallen asleep."

"What time is it?"

"Almost one. Hungry?"

"No, but—ugh." I run my tongue over my pasty teeth. A Clint Eastwood western is on the TV screen, orange-tinted film flickering on mute. "I need to brush my teeth and change."

"I'll make tea? And I have some sashimi, half price from Sakuro."

"Okay to the tea."

Mom and I don't usually follow the schedules that most other families have. Ever since I was little, bedtime has been whenever you fall asleep in the middle of whatever you're doing. Breakfast, lunch, and dinner happen when you're hungry, and the menu for those meals often gets switched around: half a leftover cheesesteak for breakfast, cereal for dinner, M&Ms and a grapefruit for lunch. Mom and I are also big fans of anything-goes omelettes, filled with whatever we unearth in the fridge or cupboard. One Thanksgiving we made them with chopped-up turkey franks because we'd forgotten about the holiday until it was too late and all the grocery stores had closed.

When I come back out to the kitchen ten minutes later, Mom has two cups of chamomile tea ready. Tuna sashimi is slabbed over some well-toasted bagels.

Mom's eyes are tired and glowing.

"Good rehearsal?" I ask, although I know the answer.

"So great. You never came, though. I knew you wouldn't," Mom adds quickly. "But everyone was asking for you." She sips her tea and it burns her mouth; she slops the cup back on the place mat. "Hot."

"Will Ken and Frannie come for opening night?"

Ken and Frannie Massara, Mom's superreligious foster parents, moved from Philadelphia down to Florida a few years ago. They sometimes come up and see

Mom in plays, although they always first make her tell them if there are dirty words or sex parts, so they can be prepared. I don't know them too well, but personally I think the Massaras are strange.

My lasting image of them is from my sixth grade graduation. They stood together, apart from everyone else in the auditorium; Frannie had cornered my teacher and was hammering her with questions about mandatory school prayer and how would you know if a student was on drugs, while Ken noisily slurped down the peanuts he'd added to the bottom of his cup of fruit punch. I was sharply aware of their loud, out-of-place presence next to the other sets of grandparents, who seemed as quiet and manageable as pet hamsters in comparison. Criticizing them makes me feel guilty though because, as Mom says, "their hearts are in the right place."

"I don't know if Ken and Frannie'd be too into the whole Shakespeare thing," Mom mused. "You know how they are—they like those musicals, stuff like *Guys and Dolls*, *Carousel*. Sing-along stuff."

"That's too bad," I say, but I'm relieved. Last time Ken and Frannie came up, at Christmas, they brought me an ugly denim purse and a frowning Jesus doll—"to share your sorrows with," Frannie had said. I hid frowning Jesus in my sweater drawer with my sorrowful Helen Keller reviews.

"Hey, Gary and I—we saw you on TV tonight, in the new five twenty-eight spot. The one with the soap bubbles," I yawn casually, watching her reaction. There is none, outside of her biting into a mouthful of raw fish and burnt bagel.

"Oh, with Brittany. That nasty dog-breath girl . . ." Her voice trails off. I wait for her to say something about Kahani's, but instead she tucks herself up on her knees and twists some of her hair around her fingers, peeling away split ends. "She calls me Susan, you know. Seven years old. And her mom just *lets* her—it's inexcusable, if you ask me."

Susan is one of those names that sounds prettier on a good-looking person and plainer on a homely person. Mom's in the first category. She's got a white apple slice of smile and pounds of soft brown hair that she hennas to a sundried tomato color, and her body is the soft curvy kind that wiggles even when she's standing still.

We have the same brown eyes and hair (although mine's the original color) and so of course people always say we look alike. I'm definitely not as pretty; it looks as though Mom's tiny, perfect features got over-cooked and blurred when they were stuck on me. And I'm unwiggly, but I'm tall—five foot ten to Mom's five foot two-and-three-quarters (although she gives herself an extra couple of inches on her driver's license). I appreciate my height, especially when Mom's having a fit about something and I can lift just my eyebrows, cross my arms, and nod down at her, like a sunflower leaning over a ladybug. Now I stretch long and stand, resting my hands on my hips.

"So," I say, giving it another shot. "Anything else interesting happen at rehearsal, or any other time, or anything?"

"Not really." Mom frowns. "I'm beat, though. I'm glad tomorrow's Tuesday and I don't have to go to Bradshaw."

"Hey, that reminds me," I say, eyeing her. "I need a new monthly train pass. Got any money? Because if not—"

"In my pocketbook." She nods absently. She stands up and starts to clear away the plate and tea mugs. "Oh, and I wanted to . . ." She clicks her tongue, like she's forgotten something. I wait expectantly. "Ty Amblin." She grins. "Did you call him? Did you ask him to the Spring Fling?"

"Oh. That." I feel my face turning pink. "No, I—see, I think I'm going to wait until later on in the week, like maybe Thursday."

"Thursday? But you have to ask him, because that gives you—hang on." Mom starts ticking off the days to the Spring Fling dance on her fingers, muttering, "Now today's the third tomorrow's the fourth Wednes—so . . . so Thursday's the sixth . . . ," but then she messes up her numbers once she hits the weekend. "Well, you should give him more than two weeks' notice," she says, dropping her hands in her lap. "Or he'll make other plans."

"Mom, two weeks is plenty, and it's not like Ty doesn't know I'm asking him. It's all pre–set up; Portia's good friends with a friend of his, and the friend, Jess Bosack, told Portia all I had to do was ask. I mean, Ty wants to go. All the Rye guys want to go to the dance." I feel like I'm talking to convince myself.

"When I was in high school, there was such a boy shortage that you had to plan quick, or you'd just get scraps."

"Well, there's no shortage at Rye, considering it's an all-guys school."

"True." Mom pushes her thumb and finger against the

inside corners of her closed eyes and rubs gently. "Take extra money and grab a to-go breakfast at the diner for tomorrow. I ate the last granola bar this morning."

"Are you sure? Will you have enough?"

"Of course." Mom gives me a curious look, and in the elastic snap of that moment I could pop out a question about Kahani's, if I were braver. But I chicken out.

"Good night, then."

"Wake me before you leave for school," she says. "Just so I know."

"Okay."

Mom can be kind of annoying that way, always wanting me to check in with her at different points in my day, making sure I'm rolling down my daily track and not spinning off in any weird, mysterious directions.

Mostly, though, there are plenty of good points to being a family of just two people, just Mom and me.

Like I never have to go on family camping trips. Portia was forced on one last year, and she said she was MBG—Majorly Beyond Grumpy—the whole time.

And a pint of ice cream and a liter of root beer splits just right for exactly two perfect root beer floats.

And we always agree on the same TV shows, like the

Monday-night movie about the call girls or serial killers instead of Monday-night football.

I chalk up Mom's eagle eye to being part of only-child/single-mom territory. And I can live with the eagle eye if it means Monday-night serial killers and no camping.

Mom seems too tired for more talking, so I decide to ask her about Kahani's sometime tomorrow.

CHAPTER

2

TUESDAY COMES AND GOES, though, and I don't even see Mom, except when I wake her up to say good-bye that morning. Some days are like that, when Mom's off to rehearsal by the time I'm home from basketball practice, and then she gets home long after I've gone to bed.

On Wednesday morning, she looks tired, and I can tell she doesn't want to go to school when she starts ordering breakfast in a foreign accent. Mom has this habit of melting into another person when she doesn't want to be where she is.

"Two sah-such, eck, an chez bees-kit, two arronch jooce, two coffee, plez," she shouts into the fast-food drive-through box.

"Sorry, ma'am," squawks the box. "Can you repeat that?"

"Come on, Mom." I slouch down in the passenger

seat and push my knees up against the glove compartment. "I'll be late—late*r*—for homeroom. I'll get a tardy slip." Of course, Mom doesn't pay me any attention.

"Two sah-such, eck—"

"I'm getting out," I threaten her. "I'll run in and order my own breakfast. I have money." Mom turns and slides her oversize sunglasses down to the tip of her nose.

"You're a little crabby this morning."

"I have a math test I need to get studying for."

Mom sighs and leans out her window. She repeats our order in a slightly more American accent.

"What is that accent, anyhow?" I grumble after we've been handed our paper bags and are chomping breakfast biscuits and slurping coffee at the traffic lights. "Sounded like some kind of Spanishy-Frenchish thing."

"Oh, it's just for fun." Mom yawns. "I should have gotten a large coffee. Rehearsal ran so late last night. I'm beat."

"When'd you get home?"

"Two, two thirty. Patsy and I went to Casa Maga for chicken nachos after."

"You should have just bagged Casa Maga knowing you have school today." I mention this for no other reason than sometimes in conversations with Mom I like to hear something logical being said.

"Shoulda woulda coulda." She yawns again.

"Besides, Mom. Isn't today the day you're presenting that Tom Sawyer musical idea?"

"Yep—aw, nuts! That reminds me." Mom slams on the brakes. I shut my lips tight at the screechy Evel Knievel sound. In the rearview mirror, I can see Lacy Finn perched like a fluffy blond spaniel in the passenger seat of her mother's white Saab. Mrs. Finn puckers her forehead, giving us an annoyed look. "I left all my notes and the script at home. Shoot shoot shoot."

"Can you present it tomorrow?"

"Nope. It took me almost two weeks to get Lemmon to agree to this appointment. I'll have to wing it. Improv. Shoot." She presses her foot on the gas as if to drive away from her mistake, and we squeal and pitch into the faculty parking lot just as the Finn car cruises past us to the student drop-off zone.

"You shouldn't go so fast in a fifteen-mile-an-hour zone."

"I don't believe you have a driver's license yet, missy."

"Don't yell at me; it was Mrs. Finn who gave you a dirty look."

"Elizabeth Finn, poster child for liposuction that she is, should butt out of my business."

I haul my bookbag over my shoulder and slam out of the car, causing the rusty hood of Old Yeller, our ancient Volkswagen Rabbit, to quiver. Whenever Mom doesn't get enough sleep, she turns stubborn against reason. The best thing to do is just to get away from her.

"Danny!" Portia jumps out of a school bus and bounds right up to my shoulder. "Are you ready for the assembly?" The assembly. I had totally forgotten.

"Don't tell me you forgot?"

"No, no, I didn't forget."

"We're presenting it right after lunch, in the upper lobby? Twelve forty-five?"

"Twelve forty-five," I repeat, taking the front stairs two at a time. "I gotta go."

"Twelve forty-five, and don't bail." She leaps away.

Portia Paulson's my best friend, but we're complete opposites. And even though I think she's the number one person after Ty Amblin I'd want to be stuck on a desert island with, the best-friendship was definitely Portia's decision. One day in second grade she kept passing me notes on her American Girls stationery and next thing I knew I was on her slumber party list and her Christmas present list.

One thing I like about Portia is how easy it is to read

her moods. Like when she gets mad, she absolutely roars, and when she's sad, tears squirt out of her eyes like watermelon seeds. Portia can't fake anything— unlike me, who will try to smile right through my meanest thought or my worst day.

Also, Portia has this knack for not letting other people's opinions matter to her. She's never the person who rolls her eyes if she's caught talking to nerds, or changes seats if she's not sitting with her friends in assembly or at the lunch table. Sometimes in tennis class Portia even voluntarily teams up with class pariah Paige Carter, who sneak-snitched on her own classmates last year when some of us wrote our Latin declensions on our wrists. The note to Mrs. Perez-Torrez was signed "Anonymous," but everyone knew.

"Paige has a great backhand," Portia says.

"Probably from all that practice backstabbing," I tell her. It was a good comeback, but the bottom line is Portia doesn't care what anyone thinks. And basically, our class respects that kind of not caring. It's why Portia's always voted class vice president, even though this year she's flunking biology and technically shouldn't hold an office. Deep down, I know I'm pretty lucky to have Portia as my best friend, since even the most stuck-up girls in my class respect her and have to think twice if they're going to say or do anything against me.

What's less lucky is how Portia counted on our friendship to bully me into taking fencing class with her for my Wednesday activity, and now there's this whole stupid assembly that is going to use all the time I'd needed to study for math. My stomach is beginning to hurt and it's not even eight thirty. I wish I hadn't drunk that coffee, which is blasting through my stomach like acid.

In homeroom, I scribble up a crib sheet to study through my morning classes, even though I'm already anticipating the usual C+. My last hope is that we have English SSR—sustained silent reading. Dr. Sonenshine lately is a big fan of SSR, because we're reading *The Odyssey,* which no one wants to finish.

"This is a boy book," the class complained after the first chapter.

"This is a classic." Dr. Sonenshine had stared like an angry owl from behind her glasses. *The Odyssey* is a real snore, although I kind of like the part about Penelope weaving and unraveling her tapestry so that those freeloading suitors can't marry her. Sometimes, Dr. Sonenshine reads sections of the book out loud in her low, twanging voice and you can feel the whole class sort of slipping back into those wine-dark sea days. But mostly we hate it.

I've gone to the Bradshaw School for Girls since kindergarten, when Mom first got her job there. Part of her salary is that I get free tuition. If you can forget about wishing that someone like Ty Amblin were around to liven up classes, a school like Bradshaw isn't as bad as it sounds. Girls get to be the captains and leaders of everything, which never happens in a school with guys in it. I'm captain of the freshman basketball team and ninth-grade student council representative, and Portia's president of the stock market club, which are all positions guys would probably snag if Bradshaw went coed.

Some people call the school "Breedshow," as a joke, I guess because the school and students look so well groomed. My public-school friends say Bradshaw's for snobs, and I guess that's my biggest complaint against Bradshaw, too. Some of the girls, like Lacy Finn and Hannah Wilder, are spoiled beyond help. The worst of them also tend to clique around together and talk about stuff like whether the skiing's better in Saint Moritz or Sun Valley. I think the day Lacy Finn found out I didn't even own a pair of skis was the same day she stopped talking to me. But that's only one type of Bradshaw girl.

There are plenty of better types, like Portia.

Mom generally likes Bradshaw, too, but she has problems with Mr. Lemmon, the fine arts director. The two don't get along even in the best of times, but lately I've heard Mom's standard pronouncement, "Dwight Lemmon is a world-class jackass," thrown around a lot, because of this spring's play. All Mom wants to do is direct this Tom Sawyer musical, but since Mom is just a part-timer, and since her loud opinions don't exactly ratchet her up to number one on Mr. Lemmon's list of favorite faculty members, he is resisting. I think she's going to wear him down, though. Last year, when Mom was the assistant director for Mr. Lemmon's deadly dull production of *Saint Joan,* she got all the Bellmont Players to come watch. If it hadn't been for them, there would have been practically no audience, so Mr. Lemmon owes her one.

"Can't you just see it?" she'll ask me whenever she's obsessing over *Tom!* which has been for a couple months now. "A bare stage, with all this—this *space* for the girls to just *express* themselves, and think of the choreography! Cartwheels, full-stage ensembles, straw hats, overalls. A play about energy. A play for athletes," she suggests, to draw me in.

Frankly, I can't see it, and I guess neither does Mr. Lemmon, whose taste runs toward more serious productions, like *Our Town* and *Inherit the Wind*.

When I read "English class is SSR, in the library" on the blackboard, I want to shout for joy. Dr. Sonenshine passes back our creative-writing essays and corrected quizzes on *The Odyssey* as we file out. She pulls me aside just as I'm priming to sprint down the hall.

"Danny, may I chat with you a second about last week's assignment? That short story you wrote, 'The Darkest Man'?"

"Um, was something the matter with it?" I feel a squirm coming on but I look at Dr. Sonenshine straight on. Mom is the master of the deadeye, go-ahead-I-dare-you face, but I'm pretty good at it, too—especially with rude salespeople and whistling construction workers.

Dr. Sonenshine's eyes widen behind her glasses. She wears her brambly gray hair caught on each side by large silver combs and her black freckles lie scattered like pepper across her brown skin. She smiles at me now.

"Not at all, Danny. Matter of fact, there was plenty that worked just fine, just fine." Her southern voice twangs banjo-style through her vowels. "And that's why when you look over my comments, and I know we've talked about this before, but with your talent, I just wish you could write something"—she exhales a papery cough into her fist—"something more true to life."

She pulls my paper from her pile and I stuff it into my book bag, not looking at the grade, to show her how I don't care. True to life. A slow burn brushes across my cheeks.

"Can I go? I need to get a library carrel."

"Go ahead." Dr. Sonenshine frowns slightly and steps aside as though I might need a lot of extra room to pass by her.

I don't take out "The Darkest Man" until I'm sitting all by myself in an upstairs carrel. Tiny squirts of red from Dr. Sonenshine's pen have rained all over the three and a half pages of my story. "Watch verb tense agreement." "New paragraph." "Pls. use spell-check." I can barely look at the tightly curled 82 in the bottom corner. A sideways-crawling comment takes up most of the page, but I don't feel much in the mood to read it. What kind of talent could I have to get an 82, a mediocre grade, a Lacy Finn and Gray Fitzpatrick kind of grade. But now there's no way I can concentrate on math. And with the fencing assembly this afternoon, I feel myself giving up (*a role that dangled entirely out of her grasp . . .*), so I stuff my books back in my book bag and leave the library. There's one thing I know I can do—my last-resort tactic.

Mom's in the faculty lounge, writing vigorously in a spiral notebook.

"Hey," I say, listing in the doorway. She looks up and raps her knuckles lightly against her forehead.

"I'm remembering everything about the Tom Sawyer pitch. Lemmon won't know what hit him. What's up?"

"I can't . . ." I wave my math book. "The test's at one fifteen, I need more time to study, I have this stupid fencing assembly I didn't practice for, I don't know what to do."

"You want a note for your teachers? Then take the train home?"

"I think so."

Mom nods and flips to a clean sheet of paper. "Back injury?"

"How about just a headache?"

"No one will believe a headache; we've used it too many times before," Mom says impatiently. Then she lowers her voice. "Look, I tell you what. Just walk out to the front hall where Ms. Luff and Dr. Polanski are. Act like you're going to get a drink of water, then just go, okay—watch."

Mom springs out of her chair and a look of unimaginable pain freezes her face. She twists her body into an S shape and her hands lurch wildly around behind her, as if searching for a knife lodged in her spine. "My back," she moans. "I think I just heard something snap or twist . . . something. Agh—there it goes again."

"Mom, they'll believe a headache, too." I glance at the door. "Cut it out, okay?"

"What have I done to my back?" she cries again, grimacing.

"Susan?" Mr. Sallese, who has been hovering out by the faculty mailboxes, dashes into the room. "Are you okay?"

"Pete, no, yes, I mean I'm fine." She straightens up. "Really. It's an old ice-skating injury."

"I have Tylenol."

"I'm fine." Mom smiles, absently rubbing the small of her back with one hand, as if the pain is subsiding.

"I didn't know you ice-skated. You know, I live right near the big duck pond out in Ivycroft. Sometime when there's some ice maybe we could—" Mr. Sallese suddenly notices me, lurking behind Mom, a giant storm cloud ready to block his sunny little proposal. I give him the deadeye.

"That might be fun, Pete." Mom's smile is unreadable.

Mr. Sallese nods and then, after another awkward moment, leaves the faculty lounge.

"Come on, Danny," Mom whispers, watching him go. "If you just say headache, they'll think you're lying."

"I'm not, anymore. It's pounding, right over my left eye."

Mom rips the piece of paper from her notebook and scratches out my standard excuse, then hands it to me with a sniff of dismissal.

"Good luck," she says.

Mr. Sallese stops me just as I'm dashing down the hall. "Your mother—you think she'll be okay?"

"Only if she doesn't exert herself too much. She really can't do things like go ice-skating anymore."

"Oh, sure, I understand." Mr. Sallese's head and Adam's apple bob together in agreement. His glance slides toward the faculty-room door, and I can tell he wants to ask me something else about Mom. I turn and run.

Over the years, lots of guys have used me to figure out Mom: what she's like, what she likes, if she likes him. Except for Warren the gemologist, who hung around a couple years—I remember he used to give me rides to school on his motorcycle when I was in fourth and fifth grade—Mom hasn't dated anyone seriously for a while.

Gary—or lots of times Elliot, before—has always been the guy who takes care of the dad responsibilities. Gary's who I take to all the father-daughter lunches, father-daughter picnics, and once even a father-daughter flag football game. Gary was pretty brave through that one. It seemed as if every time I turned around another aggressive Bradshaw dad had pounced on him and knocked him to the ground.

"Bradshaw parents haven't exactly opened their arms to the homosexual community," Gary explained when Elliot and Mom saw the bruises.

"Not yet," Elliot answered, always the optimist. That was before Elliot got sick, when they were thinking of adopting a kid since they thought they were doing such a good job helping Mom raise me.

Mom even told me once, although she wasn't supposed to, that after Elliot died Gary named me the primary beneficiary of his will, since he doesn't speak to his parents in Louisiana and doesn't have any other family.

"Don't ever say I told you. Never, never say anything about it." Mom had pressed her hand to her heart and closed her eyes dramatically, but I knew that Gary's gesture pleased her, which was why she had blurted out the secret to me in the first place. Thinking of Gary's will can give me the creeps and a safe, protected feeling both at the same time.

But it was Elliot who used to get mad whenever I came home on fake sick days or when I skipped classes with bogus notes from Mom. Since Elliot was a play and movie critic, he used to work at home, so he always knew when I cut out early. I used to have to climb the fire escape and jimmy open my bedroom window to avoid him, and even then he would catch me if the TV or radio was turned up too loud.

"School's not an optional activity, Susan," I overheard him say once.

"Don't tell me how to raise my daughter," Mom had snapped back. At the time, sitting in my room, eating mint chocolate chip ice cream, and reading magazines, I'd thought, Yeah, Elliot. Don't tell Mom how to raise me.

But days like today, as I'm sneaking out the side-door exit of the middle school lobby and then leaping like a fugitive down the road to the train station, I feel a twinge of guilt to be cutting school. And deeper inside me, there's that familiar hurt of missing Elliot, knowing that I won't ever need to sneak up the fire escape again.

CHAPTER

3

HOME.

The oven clock reads 12:16. I drop my book bag and the mail on the floor and drag myself to the couch, where I turn on the talk shows and bask in the lucky break of a March sun. Sunlight pours in through the eggshell curtains. I push my hair back from my face. Maybe I can get an early tan for the Spring Fling. I throw my legs over the arm of the sofa. Nothing's better than an unexpected day off from school.

Rick Finzimer smiles at me from the bookshelf. "Nice work cutting school, Danny," I imagine him saying. "Couldn't have planned a better escape myself. She makes it almost too easy, don't you think? But your mom always was a pushover."

"Shut up," I mutter. For some reason, I tend to imagine Rick Finzimer having this snickering, nasty personality. Who knows why; it's not like I've spent any time hanging out with the guy, and he looks friendly enough in his picture. But it makes me feel safer, I think, having this idea that my father is a little bit snarky, because it puts me off missing him. Which I guess I do, in a way—although less intensely than I miss Elliot. It's strange that Rick Finzimer's absence should bother me at all, though, because why should I miss someone I've never known?

The story of my mom and dad isn't an unusual one. They met in high school, they fell in love, she got pregnant, they eloped, I was born, they fell out of love, got divorced, and he moved away to Vermont.

When I was little he used to send me stuff: a cassette player that doesn't work anymore, a string of seed pearls, and one summer an enormous tortoiseshell from Seoul, Korea, from when he had visited there to watch the Olympics. I love my shell. It takes up an entire corner of my room and I crawl inside it with my laptop when I'm writing, although now I kind of have to squeeze to fit.

After I got older the presents stopped coming. Mom rarely talks about Rick Finzimer, but when she does, she makes him out to be this charming, brilliant guy, and his and Mom's quick trip through marriage sounds like it was as full of fights and romance as a soap opera.

"We had fun," Mom will say with a smile from time to time. "And of course, we had you. So I have no regrets."

She should have at least one regret, but I guess they must have been having too much fun the day they thought up my name, Dandelion Lark Finzimer. There's just no excuse to name a person after a weed, and they didn't even have the '60s to blame for it.

"But I adore that name," Mom told me once, dreamy eyed. "Dandelions are so magical, the way they're always changing—first so sturdy and egg-yolk yellow, then a puff of lace, until they drift away in the wind."

"It's a cartoon name," I stormed. "It just shows how you were too young to be making parentish decisions."

Dandelions describe Mom better, anyway: how she's always changing her hairstyle or her voice, shifting her personality with whichever direction her mood is blowing.

The emotions between my parents seem to have drifted into the wind, too, particularly after I was born, because Rick Finzimer keeps in absolutely no contact with Mom or me. In fact, I don't know any Finzimers at all, no aunts or uncles, no grandparents—nothing.

Mom says she never knew them that well, herself.

"But those Finzimers are a nasty crew," Mom has mentioned more than a few times. "They didn't want us to get married in the first place—thought I'd tricked him into it—and I'm sure they're perfectly happy to have no connection with us now. Their spitefulness made the divorce very tough on me. But at the end of the day, it's their loss, not getting to know you."

I can't even remember Rick Finzimer, really. In a blurry way I remember living with the Massaras, and I have a clear picture of the broiling hot summer when we moved into 4M, because Mom put a leaky plastic wading pool in the middle of our living room and the downstairs neighbors' ceiling leaked and we almost got evicted. I do have this hazy memory of a tall, blond, bearded man, but then I could just be remembering Gary during his country-western phase.

Rick Finzimer's remarried now, and he lives with his wife and kids out in California. I discovered this on my own, thanks to a little detective work.

About a year and a half ago, I dared myself to flip through the phone book, calling all the people with the last name Finzimer (there were seven, but two listings were spelled with the extra *m*) and asking for Rick, please. I got hang-ups and busy signals and weird voices on answering machines, but I kept trying and finally I connected with a lady who asked, "Big

Rick or little Ricky?" Her voice was polite and crackly.

"Little Ricky." I crossed my fingers.

"Well now, Ricky hasn't lived here for over a dozen years."

"Do you have a number or address where I could get in touch with him?" I asked. My hand was slippery on the phone.

"May I ask who's calling?"

"Yes." I read my preprinted excuse slowly off the index card. "My name is Megan Jones and I'm calling on behalf of Rick Finzimer's college. We're currently asking for alumni donations to build a new gymnasium."

"How wonderful. Hold on a minute, honey." She clunked down the receiver and I heard her talking to a man's voice in the background. When she returned, a little out of breath, she read off an address and phone number, out in Los Angeles. I copied the information carefully, and that's when she told me, in a chatty old-ladyish way, about little Ricky's dental hygienist wife and her grandkids. I wanted to ask how many kids and their names, but I got paranoid that then she'd start asking me more questions, too.

"If you want to put me down for a contribution, I'd be happy to make one," she said at the end of the call.

"Okay," I answered, and then she gave me her name, Paula Finzimer, and I took down her credit card number for a twenty-dollar donation.

"Thank you," I said.

"Good luck with your fund-raising, Megan," she answered.

She sounded so sweet it made me want to tell her, right then, who I was. But I didn't. I thanked her again and hung up the phone. Then I put on my sneakers and Walkman and shot baskets in the park for about two hours. It depressed me for a long time, realizing that the only way to have a friendly conversation with my own grandmother was if I were some dumb girl named Megan Jones. But trying to strike up a relationship with my Finzimer grandparents would not be a good idea without Mom's permission, and I don't think letting me get to know them is in her plans anytime soon.

"Oh, those horrible, spiteful, awful people—that's all in the past." She shudders when I try to work them into the conversation.

"Maybe they've mellowed out," I say. "Maybe they've gone soft."

"Flea-bitten old curmudgeons," she responds. "A pair of rotten apples." And that would be the end. It's not like me to open up a can of worms. I'm more the type who hides the unopened worm can on a back shelf in my brain, behind my New Year's resolutions.

From the phone book, I learned that my grandparents live about forty minutes away, on Poplar Avenue in Pottstown. Poplar Avenue sounds like exactly the right name for a street where grandparents live. Sometimes I like to think of them sitting out on their porch on rocking chairs, drinking bourbon or hot toddies or whatever it is old people always drink, pining for a glimpse of me, and wishing that, when they'd had the chance, they hadn't been so spiteful to their daughter-in-law.

Who knows what really caused the falling out between Mom and the Finzimers. Mom often revises her history to suit her taste, so it's hard to get a straight story out of her. Her brain contains what Mr. Spitts, our biology teacher, would call a "permeable cell wall" between facts and fiction. She's always changing story endings or beginnings or the parts in the middle. For instance, I've heard a lot of strange accounts of Mom's life in "the system" before she was permanently placed with the Massaras.

She told me about how she worked as a magician's assistant in Las Vegas. She once described living in Seattle, in an abandoned house with a bunch of illegal aliens from China. A few times she told me about how she and a friend camped out in a department store in Newark, New Jersey for almost three months, dining on the candy, nuts, and dried fruit they stole from the glass cases, and sleeping on the showroom beds. She wasn't placed with the Massaras until she was fourteen, but she gives them credit, she says, for somehow getting her to finish high school. My guess is that they temporarily put the fear of God into her, which has been proven to work on plenty of people.

Sometimes Mom's stories change, like instead of being a magician's assistant she worked stacking chips at a casino roulette wheel. It's as though she's always writing and revising a different script for her life, but at least the stories are interesting.

That call to my grandmother bugged me because it ended up being so useless and dumb, after all my hoping. I thought up other ways I would have liked the conversation to have turned out. I imagined the crackly voice growing quiet, then in a hopeful whisper saying, "I know that voice. There's no mistaking the voice of a Finzimer. Is this my long lost grandchild? Is this Ricky's firstborn daughter talking to me?" Eventually I managed to shove the whole bad experience out of my thoughts. Inventing scenarios was better left to Mom.

Of course I never told Mom what I did, and I never called Rick Finzimer's California number, since it would have shown up on the AT&T bill.

I did finally get up the nerve to write him a letter, about eight months ago. It was a simple card that said, "Hi how are you, school is great, Mom is fine, sometimes I think about you and I hope you don't mind that I looked up your number." In my P.S. I added, "Please don't feel like you have to write back. I understand how life can get pretty hectic—it will probably take me another week just to find a stamp to mail this card!!!"

Life must be pretty hectic all the time for Rick Finzimer, because I've never heard from him. There are times when I feel stupid about that card and wish I hadn't added all those dumb girlie exclamation points. Other times I think about it and wonder why I care whether or not Rick Finzimer contacts me. After all, I'd grown up with Mom and Gary and Elliot all swarming around me, so it's not as if I ever lacked for parenting. It's the not knowing that eats at me, I guess. The unsolved mystery of the man in the picture.

The bagels are more freezer-burned than ever when I drag myself off the couch to make my peanut butter and jelly sandwich. There's only an empty orange juice container in the fridge, so I drink tap water and after lunch I'm full of enough energy to read Dr. Sonenshine's comments on my creative writing essay.

The Darkest Man

He hung by his talonlike fingers onto the side of the steep glass mountain, a bold smile playing over his lips. The Darkest Man. No one knew his name, but when the simple townsfolk saw his silhouette outlined against the Dvorkian sky, they were filled with dread. The Darkest Man.

What sounded so eerie a couple of weeks ago now just seems silly and immature. Dr. Sonenshine was probably right to slap me that 82. I skip through the story to her comments.

Danny, you have really managed to create a strange and fascinating world in the science fiction/fantasy genre. I wish I could go to a place like Dvorkia, especially during all this cold weather! I do think, however, that the character of "The Darkest Man" remains somewhat elusive. It would be interesting if you could develop a story based on characters and events that are more relevant to your own life. Also, please remember to run your work through spell-check and watch your verb tense agreement.

The phone rings and I let the machine get it. "Danny, pick up if you're there." Portia's voice is angrily insistent. "I know you're home. Your mom said you left with back spasms. Thanks a lot; I know it was just to get out of fencing, which went really bad without you." She sighs, a loud leaf-rustling noise over the tape.

"Anyhow, Lauren and I're going to watch the Rye junior varsity wrestling matches, and I really hope she doesn't ask Ty Amblin to the Fling before you? Because she said she maybe was going to? So uh . . . so call me tonight, anyway. Oh, and uh, I have something important to talk about." She slams down the phone.

"Doubtful," I mutter. Portia rarely has anything important to talk about. And Lauren already asked Drew Brewer to the dance. Portia's lies are almost too easy to catch.

I scoop the mail off the floor. The March issue of *The Lilac* is in and now I've given myself enough time to prepare myself to flip through it. I know in a minute that my story's not in there, and I'm mad at myself for searching for it.

"Car Crazy," "Let Sleeping Dogs Wake," "Disengaged," "Julio Underwater," "Soap." I read through the table of contents very slow, wishing for the words "Woodpile Baby"—my story's title—to surface suddenly with the others.

Nothing.

I flip to "Car Crazy," by Mark Gould. "Mike cared for his Ferrari better than his women," I read out loud.

Stupid story. Fifth place.

"Woodpile Baby" has a way more interesting idea—all about this orphanage in olden times where babies got dropped off in the middle of the night, placed on top of the woodpile by their poor mothers who couldn't care for them. One night a baby freezes to death and her ghost haunts the school, eventually setting fire to it. The end has everyone burning right up to a crisp, even the nice cleaning lady. It's a very tragic, Stephen King–ish kind of story.

"Gruesome and depressing," Mom had said, but she let me send in a check to cover the five-dollar entry fee. Mom never thinks my entry fees are a waste of money, even though I've never won anything. "Let the world know you're in it," is her motto.

Winning submissions will be notified, the rules explained vaguely.

I hadn't been notified. I hadn't even been honorable mentioned.

My head really does hurt.

There's only one aspirin in the medicine cabinet, so I swallow it and replace the empty bottle. At least the people at *The Lilac* who probably were all laughing scornfully at "Woodpile Baby" don't know my real name. Whenever I enter a contest I use my pen name, Antonia de Ver White. It's a name for how I picture a serious writer: a chain-smoking older woman with high cheekbones and a knowing laugh.

I know it's a babyish thought, but I'm thinking of switching my name permanently to Antonia de Ver White, when I get to college. I mentioned this once privately to Dr. Sonenshine, since she's a writer on the side, too, and she said some Native Americans get new names when they become men and women, so if I wanted to change, why not?

The phone rings again. I walk slowly out of the bathroom to watch the machine take the call. "Pick up, it's Mom." I pick up.

"Hey."

"How's your head?"

"I'll be okay. You're the one who has Mr. Sallese thinking you used to be in Ice Capades."

"He's a nice guy. The kids seem to like him, too."

"Whatever. By the way, we're out of aspirin."

"I'll get some on the way home. Guess what? Lemmon thumbs-upped Tom Sawyer, and I'm the primary director. Do you know how long I've been waiting for this chance?"

"Yeah; that's so cool, Mom." I can hear her smile at

the end of the line.

"He said it was my neck on the line or my head on the block or whatever that expression is, so I think he hopes it'll be a big disaster and I'll get canned. And who knows, maybe he's right. I already feel out of my element."

And then for some reason, maybe because so much of the day has already turned into mush, because of *The Lilac* or Dr. Sonenshine's comments or the back-spasm thing or the fast-food accent or the math test or Portia's mean message red-blinking on the answering machine, I blurt out exactly the last thing I want to deal with right now.

"The stakes are pretty high with the Kahanis selling their whole business."

I want to hang up on the silence that fills the other end of the line. I want to take back my snippy words immediately. But I'm quiet. I stand with the phone jammed against my ear and wait.

"Gary told you?" Mom's voice is calm, flat as milk.

"Why didn't you?"

"Because. I have a lead on a new job. Because I want-ed to wait till I had a new job."

"And, so okay, so you have something? . . ." I shift from one leg to another, trying to figure out Mom's way of thinking. A new job. A new, secret job.

"Yeah, I might."

"Well, what is it? Tell me."

"Later, maybe. When I get home. Maybe." Her voice is defensive and a little abrupt.

"Don't feel like you have to do me any favors," I say half jokingly.

"What do you mean by that?"

"Nothing, I guess. See you later."

"Yeah." She clicks off. I stare at the phone in my hand for a few seconds. "You don't even own a pair of ice skates," I say to the dial tone.

The conversation confused me, like I was just in some weird play and didn't know my lines. It annoyed me, too. One of the problems about being in a family of two is that if something goes wrong between me and Mom, there's no one else to fall back on, no dad or brother or sister to find and ask, "What's wrong with Mom? Why is she acting so sad or mysterious or irritating?" And even if they can't tell you, at least you can hang out with an ally who will say comforting things to you like, "Oh, you know Mom, that's just how she gets sometimes."

I look over at the photo of Rick Finzimer. "That's just how she gets sometimes," I say.

CHAPTER
4

THE LENOXVILLE LOCAL runs northwest from Philadelphia, making station stops starting in Foxwood and ending all the way out in cow country, Lenoxville, with nine stops in between. I live in Foxwood, where foxes and woods both are long gone. Foxwood's right in the city outskirts of ugly, crooked roads, neon-lit fast-food restaurants, and colonies of row houses guarded by gap-railed wooden porches.

Portia lives in Saint Germaine, which is about twenty-five minutes away from me and walking distance to the Saint Germaine Hunt Club, where they still have foxes, in addition to people who are rich enough to hunt them down. Saint Germaine is full of golf clubs, country clubs, and cricket clubs, and the Paulsons have memberships to all of them. Portia and I rotate eating lunches on her parents' different club charge accounts. Mom and Gary like to use Saint Germaine as an example of how perfectly nice kids can grow up to to be spoiled and Republican, but I don't think Portia's turning out too bad. If I had kids, I'd want to bring them up somewhere exotic, like Australia or Paris, so that they'd have cute accents, but Saint Germaine is definitely an option, too. It certainly wins over Foxwood.

I buy a round-trip off-peak ticket with change that I scraped from under the couch and out of Mom's and my coat pockets, and I jump on the train to Saint Germaine. Then I walk the half mile from the station to Portia's house. The sun's disappearing into a cold, cloud-chalked sky, and over my sweatshirt I'm only wearing Gary's thin hand-me-down barn jacket. Mustard Moss, the catalog had called this color, which in real life is closer in hue to Old Canned Peas.

"Danny. Good to see you're out of traction." Portia smirks, but the meanness of her machine message leaks out of her voice when she sees me looking so apologetic. "How're you feeling?"

"Okay. Can I come in?" I bounce up and down on my toes to show her how cold it is. There's a low whirring noise drifting from upstairs and I give Portia a puzzled look as I step inside the front hall.

"Dad." She shakes her head. "He just bought one of

those NordicTracks for the exercise room? Since his doctor told him, remember, about his heart?"

"Those are cool, I've seen those on TV." I follow Portia out to the kitchen, where Mrs. Jackson, the housekeeper, is chopping carrots.

"Hi, Mrs. Jackson," I say.

"Hi," she answers, and for the millionth time I wonder if Mrs. Jackson knows my name. Portia says of course she does, but I'm not so sure.

Portia immediately starts setting an extra place at the butcher-block table. We've been friends long enough for her to know that when I come over at suppertime, chances are I'll want to eat. A lot. She's also seen how Mom and I shop for food.

"You're the only two people I know who do all their grocery shopping at the 7-Eleven," she said once. "Seriously, when's the last time you were even inside a real grocery store?" As if Portia's ever had to do the family grocery shopping. The Paulson family is so insanely rich that they even have a lady come to decorate their house at Christmastime. "Holiday coordinator," Mrs. Paulson explained to me once. "Not an interior designer." Like this distinction messes people up all the time.

"So, let's hear it? One good reason why you cut

school today?" Portia stands with her hands on her hips. Portia always forces you to be a hundred percent up front, but on the flip side, she doesn't hold grudges.

"I had to skip out, Portia." I try to smother the whine in my voice. "I needed an extra day to study for math." Which I hadn't even given a thought to cracking into yet.

"Your mom lets you get away with way too much."

"I know." I hope I look guilty enough.

"Well strike up the band, here's Miss Dand!" Mr. Paulson strides through the kitchen, looking like Kermit the Frog in his green fleece warm-ups. He gives me a kiss that leaves a wet splotch on my forehead.

"Ew, Dad." Portia rolls her eyes. "I'm sure Danny loves you kissing her all sweaty and disgusting?"

"She's not allergic," Mr. Paulson answers. "Right, Dand?"

"Uh-uh." I look down and fiddle with the edge of the place mat. Every time I'm around other people's dads I find myself acting stupid, like my regular self defected to a lump in my throat and only the words of some-body way more boring can get dislodged. Mr. Paulson makes me feel especially quiet, since I think he's funny and friendly and I like the way he always smacks a kiss on my head like I'm in his real family.

"Anyway, Dad, Danny and I were right in the middle of a crucial conversation?"

"Oh, and what's the trauma du jour at Bradshaw?" Mr. Paulson laughs. He moves to the wet bar and pulls out a martini glass and a silver shaker and strainer. "Some poor feckless soul chip a nail? Someone get denied her gold card privileges?"

"Daa-aad, come on. And maybe you better forget about that martini?" Portia wags her finger at him. "I hear Mom."

Once Mrs. Paulson swings into the kitchen, there's no more time for me to talk to Portia about fencing. Mrs. Paulson just takes over a room. She used to be a Laker Girl or Dallas Cowgirl or some kind of professional cheerer, and she still has a lot of spins and kicks left in her, not to mention a peppy voice that's always on megaphone volume.

"Dan-dee-lightful! I swear you've grown another inch since last time I saw you. Chaz, is that a martini? You know better, what did Dr. Little say?" Mrs. Paulson spins over to her husband and spears an olive from his glass with one perfect blade of nail, then spins over to Mrs. Jackson. "Oh, Sharon, dinner looks great! And Danny's staying? Great! It's all low cal, low fat, low cholesterol. Even

the salad dressing. Chaz isn't my young bull anymore."
She winks at me. Considering Portia's the daughter of
Mr. Paulson's third marriage, I wonder if Mrs. Paulson
even knew Mr. Paulson when he was a young bull. He
has to be more than fifteen years older than she is.

"Ew, Mom, that's so disgusting?" Portia sighs, sitting
in her seat and snapping open her napkin. "Young bull?
Grotesque. Who are you? Saying that with your own
daughter right at the table? I'm just glad Carter's still at
track practice." Carter is Portia's younger brother, who's
a twit and luckily is almost always at sports practices.
Mrs. Paulson just winks at me again.

"And Dad, are you possibly thinking about a shower
before dinner?" Portia wrinkles her nose.

"Not even entertaining the concept." Mr. Paulson
smirks. Portia sighs with disgust. I sit and reach for the
not very low cal–looking buttered mashed potatoes.

Mom once told me that she hates the ceremony of
dinners, that when she lived with the Massaras, Frannie
would spend hours toiling over her cookbooks trying to
get her meatloaf perfect, and that the table would have
to be set with cloth napkins and Ken would say about
forty minutes of grace—all for five minutes' worth of
eating. After dinner, it was Mom's job to clean up the

kitchen, which ate up another half hour since there was no dishwasher. She told me this story the day we bought our own dishwasher, at fifty percent off from Kahani's. We never have to use that dishwasher more than a dozen times a year, but I guess it makes her feel safe.

When I listen to the noises of the Paulsons' dinner, though, there is something about the clink and scrape of forks and knives, the friendly words—*will you pass me this or that? mmm, this tastes good, I like this better broiled, fried, with creamed spinach, without butter, yes, it's healthier that way*—that makes me want to bring Mom over to Portia's house, sit her down at the table with us, and say, "See, Mom, sometimes it's not so bad to set out utensils, even ones that you might not need, and to use cloth napkins, and to have an extra dish for peas instead of smacking the pot right on the table." I bet Mom wouldn't mind a sit-down dinner every once in a while, especially since the Massaras wouldn't be there praying over their food, and since we have a dishwasher.

Mrs. Jackson finishes bringing out the rest of the dishes and then she disappears to somewhere else in the house. She and her husband, who takes care of the Paulsons' lawn and the garden, live in a little house on the Paulson property.

Portia's family doesn't seem to mind, but it would make me feel weird if people lived on my land in a little house while I hogged up the big gorgeous one, like serfs and lords from medieval times. I just always hope that Mrs. Jackson takes comfort in the fact that Mrs. Paulson has filled her home with just about the ugliest furniture I ever saw; she even has zebra wallpaper in her dressing room. Although I know I could live with zebra wallpaper if my living room were as big as the school gym.

Mr. and Mrs. Paulson are the kind of parents who make their kids tell them every single thing that happened to them from the minute they woke up to the second they sit down to dinner. And even though Portia complains about how many questions they ask her, once she gets going, listing off each hour of her existence on the planet, no detail is too small. Lots of her stories go, "And so then I said? no wait first Jess said?—oh, hang on, let me get this right."

All through dinner, I try not to squirm from restlessness, but secretly I'm thinking that when I have kids, I'll never let them make me suffer like this. At least Carter's not around. He talks in rambly circles, too, plus he stutters and his days are even less interesting than Portia's.

"Now, Danny, I seem to recall that you're taking Ty

Amblin to the Spring Fling next month. Is that right?"
Mr. Paulson asks once Portia's finished telling all about
the fencing assembly and what a disaster it was, mostly because she had to be Kathleen Comber's partner
since I wasn't there.

"I haven't asked him yet," I say. "He might say no."

"Oh, good grief." Mr. Paulson flicks his fingers dismissively. "He'd be an imbecile to pass up the opportunity. The real question is, is Ty Amblin good enough for
you? Is he a worthy date for *you?*"

I give a shrug that's meant to show how I wouldn't
really care if Ty's a good enough or a worthy enough
date for me or not.

"I mean it, Danny girl," Mr. Paulson continues.
"When young men aren't busy acting like jerks, they're
usually being imbeciles; I know because I was one
myself, long ago. I've never met this Ty Amblin, but I
hope he's a solid, quality young man."

"Dad, what's your deal? It's not like Danny needs
your okay, okay?"

"No, it's all right," I break in. "I mean," I say, turning to
Mr. Paulson, "Ty's a nice, um, quality guy. He is. I guess."

"Good." Mr. Paulson leans back in his chair and
looks at Portia. "One day you'll be a protective parent,

too, my dear. To your kids and anybody else's. That's just how the game works."

"I'm going to be a cool mom, like Danny's," Portia says. "One who would let me get a tattoo." Mr. Paulson just smiles. They've been through the tattoo argument a dozen times, and I'm happy that Mr. Paulson doesn't take the bait.

After dinner we head up to Portia's room, which is like stepping inside a scooped-out cantaloupe. Even the lights are soft and peach tinted, and the mirrors over the dressing table smooth out your face so that you can sort of imagine yourself in a fashion magazine. I know some kids at school think Portia's slightly vain, but with mirrors like these, it would be hard not to think you look pretty great all the time.

"So we need a Ty Amblin strategy, pronto, or you're going to be hanging out in serious loser mode, eating graham crackers at the chaperons' table. First, some visual aids." Diving under her bed, Portia hoists up the Rye yearbook that she stole out of Carter's room and flips to page sixty-eight, which has last year's eighth-grade class pictures. "Could he be any cuter? Survey says, no chance."

"You know I have the RTs for that picture," Even

though Ty's giving the Smile, a closed slip of grin that catches one corner of his mouth higher than the other, looking at his elf ears makes my arm hairs stand on end. RTs are short for Retard Tingles, which is what you get when someone else is being or doing something so dorky that you feel tingly with embarrassment for them. Portia and I shortened to abbreviations when Mrs. Jackson yelled at us that you shouldn't use the word *retard,* because it wasn't politically correct. It was one of the only times I ever heard Mrs. Jackson yell.

"RTs? Because of his crooked part?"

"No, because of that elf shadow made from his ears." But now his part looks stupid, too. I slam the book shut and shiver. Anything related to Ty Amblin always gives me a way more intense reaction than I expect. "I haven't made up my mind to invite him, you know. He looked, like, so twitty when I saw him with his mom at Strawbridge's. In that goofy pink—"

"I know, you've already said, that pink golf sweater. But I mean, Ty really plays golf? It's not like he's wearing it for, like, modeling purposes? His family owns a place in West Palm, and he gets special golf lessons from the pros and stuff."

"Honestly, though. Do you really see me hanging out

with a guy who wears a pink golf sweater?" But all this talking about Ty catches a little thrill in different parts of me, in my fingertips and behind my neck and low in my spine.

I've had a thing for Ty since fourth grade, when he came to the annual Rye/Bradshaw Switchover Day and I was assigned as his Bradshaw Buddy. He had soft yellow hair and soft manners and soft little fingernails rounded into china-doll half-moons, so much nicer than my inky, raggedy ones. Then a couple years later, his parents rented a house in Nantucket near Portia's parents' house, and we all spent the summer playing tennis and traveling in packs with other local kids to the only movie theater in town. Later, in seventh grade, Ty and I danced every dance at the annual end-of-the-year Rye/Bradshaw Middle School Mixer.

It doesn't seem like a lot, but when you go to a school that's all girls or all guys, even the smallest encounters count way more than if you saw that person at school every day.

"There's like a ten percent chance he's coming to our basketball game tomorrow. Jess told me. You could ask him then?"

"I'd rather call than do it in person. You can't hang up if you're getting rejected face-to-face."

"Stop, you're so insecure. If you don't hurry up and invite him, someone else will, or he'll be going to the civic center for that boring Bulls game."

"Bulls games are *so* not boring," I snap. Sometimes Portia gets too girlish, and I hate being called insecure. "I'd majorly go see the Bulls over this dumb dance if I had the chance."

"Yuck, how can you even—"

"Hey, I just remembered something," I interrupt. Arguing with Portia about basketball isn't worth the time it takes. I lift myself off Portia's melon-ruffled bed and sit at her dressing table, uncapping one of her dozens of lip liners. I carefully start outlining my mouth. "You said earlier you had important news."

"I did?" Portia flips through a magazine. "Oh please, oh puh-leez let me lose at least ten pounds by next Saturday to fit into my Vera Wang."

"Yeah, you did. Remember? On the answering machine."

I can see Portia reflected in the mirror. She's pushed in and is kneading her lips over her braces, scraping the soft skin of her mouth over the metal. It hurts, she told me, but she does it to put more poutiness in her lips.

"Stop doing that thing with your mouth, okay, and

just tell me."

"What thing?" She stops doing it, though, and flips her hair into her face. It splashes heavily over her eyes and she drags her fingers through it, flipping it first to one side, then the other. Gold and honey brown streaks catch the lamplight and swirl together like a shampoo ad. Portia's hair practically has its own personality.

"Come on." I deadeye her and she pulls up to sit on her knees, flipping the magazine to the side.

"Okay, it's about your mom."

"My mom?"

"See, I saw her . . . last night? At the Greenhouse? I was out to dinner with Mom and Dad. Danny, I had no idea."

I knew it. Mom went on a secret date with Mr. Sallese. He'd been just a bit too friendly with her in the faculty lounge. The Greenhouse is a pretty popular bar and grill restaurant; it's where Bradshaw girls throw their sweet sixteen parties and where the senior class dinner usually is held. Mom had been sort of mysterious last night about what she was doing. She told me she had rehearsal every night this week, but thinking back on it, rehearsal every night seems like an intense schedule, even for a last-minute Rosalind/Celia switch.

But Mr. Sallese is awful. He's shorter than I am, not

counting the huge helmet of Ken-doll hair that swoops up from his forehead. He has a son, too, named Rocco. I didn't even think that was a real name. Worse, Rocco plays drums in a grunge band. I see my whole new step-familied life in a flash and it looks crowded and horrifying.

"He's nice, Mr. Sallese." I shrug.

"Okay, I totally understand if you want to change the subject? Mr. Sallese, yeah, he's nice, but he definitely mousses."

I'm confused. "Wait, Portia, how'm I changing the subject?"

"And anyone trying for that much volume? That might mean hair plugs."

"Portia, hang on—who was my mom with at the Greenhouse on Tuesday?"

Portia looks straight at me, her eyes round as dimes. She seems nervous.

"With? No, Danny—she wasn't with anyone. She was, uh, training? To be, uh, a waitress? I think? I'm pretty sure."

"Oh, yeah, that." My brain freezes but I keep right on talking. "I only know a little about that, but she's, like—it's some acting thing, technique thing. She's in a new play." My heart is beating sickeningly fast, and I wonder if fourteen-year-olds ever have heart attacks.

"Ohhh." Portia looks visibly relieved. "A play about a waitress? That sounds cute. Because it would be kind of funny—strange funny I mean?—if she really was waitressing? Since, well, since so many of us kids go, since so many people go out to dinner at the Greenhouse, you know? You know what I mean?"

"Yeah." I shove myself into my barn jacket. "Look, I better head home."

"Okay, yeah, I need to study bio. And Mr. Jackson'll give you a lift to the station. It's totally dark now."

"See, Mom gets into method acting. She's read all that Uta Hagen stuff."

"Well, then I guess that would be good training and since it's not for real—Danny, I hope you don't mind, but can I just tell you?" Portia smiles and presses her fingers to her braces as if she's trying to hold inside something she wants to shout. Instead she giggles. "Your mom is about the most clueless waitress that I ever ever saw."

I laugh. Right now it's just about one of the most unfunny things I've heard in a long time, but I laugh anyway. "Yeah I bet," I say. "Some things you just can't act, probably."

And then I escape.

*   *   *

The train, crowded a couple hours ago, holds only a handful of businessmen and women heading home from their jobs. They sit in their overcoats and gray suits and the sounds they make are all muted and polite. A quiet crinkle as they turn the page of a newspaper, a discreet ahem when they clear their throats. I hear one man talking on his cell phone, his hushed voice explaining what time he'll be pulling into the station. A few of them give me quietly thoughtful looks, like they're trying to figure out what I'm doing on their train.

Small mysteries are lifting all at once from my brain like a cloud of gnats. The pair of ugly black sneakers that Mom had been carrying around in her basket bag this past week. The dried ketchup smear on her jeans, grossly big and sloppy, even for Mom. The time I tried calling Bellmont to remind her to pick up orange juice and Louis said she wasn't scheduled to come in that night. "I was there," Mom had said later, looking mystified. "I was in the box office. Louis sure is losing it lately."

It seems so strange and terrible, thinking of her hiding this job from me. What did it mean? Why wouldn't she have discussed this with me before? I feel sort of worthless, knowing that for some reason Mom decided

I didn't count enough to confide in about her decision.

"Bide Away," the conductor calls.

Worthless. Mr. Paulson asked if Ty Amblin was worth my time. I'd never thought about it before. Now I wonder if Mom sees me as a worthwhile person. A person you can explain important things to, even if they're tough to talk about, like losing your job and having to work as a waitress. I bet if Mr. Paulson lost his job and had to work as a bartender or something, he'd tell Portia. Mr. Paulson was always trying to explain bonds and debt origination to Carter and Portia, no matter how much they whined to him that they didn't get it. He thinks it's worth his time, sharing stuff about his job with his kids.

It's funny, how Mr. Paulson always knows those details about my basketball and guys and whatever's going on at Bradshaw. He's a really great dad; I always feel bad when Portia acts rude to him, and I like to think that part of Mr. Paulson secretly wishes that I were his daughter.

The man sitting across from me wears a slouchy gray hat that keeps slipping over his eyes. His face in profile seems tired but friendly. I imagine him turning around. Our eyes lock and there's a moment of recognition.

"Danny," he says. His throat catches in a laugh of

disbelief. "My darling daughter, I've been looking everywhere for you."

"Didn't you get my letter?" I falter.

"Ah, no, my horrible second wife must have ripped it up. She's insane with jealousy over my persisting memories of Susan. No matter, I'll be getting rid of her soon." He smiles cryptically. "It's so good to see you."

"Dad, Mom and I could seriously use your help right now."

Gray-hat man suddenly shifts and looks over at me, startled. "Did you say something?"

"Oh! No, I mean," I shake my head quickly, "I just wondered if you had the time."

"It's seven fifty-eight," he says, obviously relieved to stare at his watch and not me.

Mom's not at the apartment when I get home, but messy traces of her presence remain. The stereo's on; a half empty can of Coke and a new bottle of aspirin stand next to a crumpled paper bag on the table; and all the cupboards are open from her last-minute dinner search. I look inside the refrigerator and find a note:

Danny,
I'm at Bellmont but won't be home till late. There's ten

dollars on my bureau for pizza. Study for math!

Love, Mom

I call Bellmont.

"She's on for tomorrow, not tonight," says Patsy. "You want her whole schedule?"

"Yeah, okay."

I write out the schedule and fold the paper in my pocket. Then I tug out the phone book, which we'd been using to steady a missing leg of the couch, and dial the number for the Greenhouse.

"Susan Finzimer, please." I disguise my voice low like a guy's.

"Jusasec, hon, I'ma transfer you over to the kitchen." There's a click and another breathless, "Hold on." The background noises sound like someone's crashing plates and silverware to the floor and then, blaring close enough in my ear so there's no doubt in my mind, Mom's voice is shouting,

"Hello? Hello? Hello?"

I hang up.

She doesn't want to tell you because she's ashamed. She doesn't want to tell you because she's afraid you'll be ashamed. The thoughts cyclone through my brain and refuse to die.

I punch in Gary's number. This is one of those times when I really need to have somebody say, "Oh, you know your mom; that's just the way she is. She can be a bit nutty." But instead I get his answering machine. I don't leave a message.

"It's so incredibly stupid of her." I lie, stomach down, on the couch. "Not to tell me. Like I can't handle it or something. What is she thinking?" And even as I'm saying all these things out loud, I'm wondering what I do think about it. Because it's flat-out awful, this image of Mom at the Greenhouse. I see her running around slopping food in front of other people, having to be nice to them if parts are burnt or cold or too spicy, counting tips against our rent.

"She'll quit in a week," I predict, addressing the photograph of Rick Finzimer. "You know Mom. She's scheming up a better plan."

But there's no one here to assure me. Rick Finzimer just smiles carelessly, keeping his thoughts, as always, to himself.

CHAPTER

5

FOUL SHOTS AREN'T ALL in the flick of your wrist, or in the way you plant your feet at the throw line. They aren't exactly about the height of the jump or the bend of your knees or the angle of your elbows, either. In my mind, a foul shot is all about timing: the one pivotal moment of release. It's a moment when your brain and your body flex together, like when you've swung up to the highest point you can go on a swing and, right before you begin to fall in a long, swooping arc back to earth, you're inside a tiny breathless instant when time stops and your heart stops and your thoughts stop and all around you, life is frozen silent.

If I can make my shot right in the middle of that kind of untouched moment, I know as soon as the ball glides into the air that the point is mine.

We're in the final minutes of the fourth quarter and the scoreboard has been clamped with a pair of 47s, a tie for us and Perry. I grip the ball. I hold my breath, bend my knees, give a last, assured fingertip squeeze. And then, right as I'm about to release the ball from my possession, I see Ty Amblin standing with his friends Jess Bosack and Scott McKinlin, right by the open doors.

And then the ball is gone, spinning out through the air, while the crowd, all eyes and stopped breath, follows its path from my hands to where it bounces off the edge of the basket. A disappointed groan rises in the bleachers. Timing. I waited too long, let my crucial moment get swallowed by the distraction of a clump of stupid guys.

I can't look at Ty and am thankful when a Perry girl grabs the ball and starts driving it downcourt, throwing us into a tight brace of guarding panic. They score, one of the 7s flips to a 9, and there's a polite murmur from the bleachers. The time buzzer sounds worse than ten fire drills in my ear.

I walk slowly over to the bench to grab my towel and water bottle, my head down to avoid eye contact. Our coach, Mrs. Sherman, yells something at me like "Buck up, kiddo"—she's always on everyone's case about being a better sport and a good loser. I feel empty, my mouth tastes like sweat and dust (*lacks not only zim but also zam, zip, and any emotion in between . . .*), and the defeat drags my body into a slumpy depression. When I lose a game, I don't care how I look to my teammates or to the other team. You lost. You're a loser. That's all I'm thinking.

Parents have swarmed in from their seats to collect girls and towels and sports bags, and I'm disappointed Mom's not here; she's usually around to see my games. She would rehash the details, revising key moments to her own Mom-vision, so that my mistakes wouldn't be all my fault, and part of me wouldn't believe her and part of me would be able to listen and laugh and maybe relax a little.

"Danny!" Portia waves from across the court and races over. "Guess who's here?" she hisses loudly and wetly in my ear. "Your very own potential mutual Spring Flinger?"

I check out of the corner of my eye. Ty must have hit the vending machines; with one hand he's glugging down raisins from the box straight into his mouth while the other holds a can of Sprite. "You want me to go over there with you?"

"Look, I was just going to call him tonight," I protest weakly. Portia squishes up her nose, irritated with me.

"Dummy, why would you want to call him if he's standing twenty feet away from you? We'll both go. It's not like we don't know those guys; you're being so insecure, especially since I've already asked Jess."

"I am not being insecure, just because I don't want to follow your plan."

"But the conversation will go much better in a group, especially since you're BNT-cubed."

Which stands for Bringing Nothing to the Table, acting like deadweight. Right now, this is probably true. Portia scoops her hair high up in her hands and lets it fall—whoosh—over her jacket. Jess Bosack looks over.

"But I'm all sweaty . . . and I just lost the game." I rub my nose and then suddenly flash Portia a big fake smile in case anyone's watching and sees me looking insecure. "And by the way, if you grab my arm and start dragging me over there like a spaz," I speak quietly behind my tightly locked teeth, "I will kill you and that's a promise."

"Like I would really do that?" Portia shakes back her hair.

"Calling's better for me, anyway. If I go now, Ty won't know that I've seen him. The late bus is going to be leaving any minute."

Then I dash away from Portia, out of the gym, into the cold air. The empty bus is waiting at the curb, and I thump down into my favorite seat, the one with the bump that the tire fits under. I press my face against the window; my skin feels stiff with salt and my ponytail elastic hugs a tangled mat of brown.

Thu-thu-thunk. My eyes fly open to see Ty knocking against the glass with the heel of his hand. He jerks his thumb to the bus door and I nod, trying not to let myself seem too energized by his presence.

"Hey, you." He smiles as he walks down the aisle. His cheeks have blossomed pink from the cold and his school tie dangles out of his camel's hair overcoat. I brush my hair in front of my chest in case of a hive attack. "Good game."

"Not really. Where were you? I didn't see you." I lift my eyebrows and pretend to stifle a yawn. Ty slides into the seat in front of me, kneeling on it backward to face me and resting his arms across the seat back.

"I was watching you from the door. We didn't get there till fourth quarter. I came to see Hannah. Hannah Wilder, you know. She's my cousin."

"On your mom's side?"

"Huh?" Ty reaches up and unlatches his window and squeaks it down, allowing a shot of cold air to blow inside.

"Cousin on your mom's—like, is your mom sisters with her mom or something?" At first Ty just stares at me and I can't tell if he doesn't get it or he's just bored by my awful BNT-cubed conversation skills.

"Hannah's dad is my uncle Craig," he says quickly, and then, thankfully, he slides on the Smile, probably to let me know that I haven't totally blown it with him yet. "So what's going on with you, Danny? Besides hoops?" Ty pulls a pack of gum out of his pocket; it's the weird no-name brand of another Bradshaw vending machine purchase. He offers me a stick, which I accept.

"Not much." I swallow. "Same old same old." I hope I don't look like I'm shivering. And then I realize how idiotic I am to feel so jumpy. Ty Amblin is probably sitting here waiting for me to ask him to the dance. He knows I'm going to, and he wants to go. I don't have to be nervous at all. My asking rushes out all at once, words clear and simple as bubbles. He nods, and flashes the Smile at me again.

"When is it?" he asks. As if he doesn't know.

"Next Saturday. And I'm pretty sure Jess and Portia are going."

"Well, yeah, sure. Sounds cool." He brushes his fingers through his soft yellow hair and nods. "Cool," he says again.

"And Jess's older brother might be able to give us all a lift, if you guys want to meet up with us at Portia's before the dance." The plan behind this casual sentence actually involved hours of phone conversation with Portia, since Mr. Paulson's so strict about putting his personal stamp of approval on our dates. Ty nods, satisfied, and lifts himself up from the seat, his two thumbs whipping at the seat back in a little drumroll. After all this anticipation, it's turned out to be a snap. Well, maybe a couple snaps.

"Great. Look forward to it. See you later then," he says. "I gotta go. My friends are waiting." He waves his hand vaguely in the direction of the gym.

"See ya." And I'm glad to see him go, glad to get back to the business of breathing normally again. A few other girls are pushing onto the late bus just as Ty gets off, and their impressed glances over at me fill me with a happy smugness inside. At least I can count one victory tonight.

"I did it," I tell Mom the next morning as we're eating breakfast at the Taste of the Town diner. "I asked Ty and he said yes."

"Fantastic." Her eyes rest soft over me. "Your dad and I went to my senior spring formal together, in high school. He wore this beautiful paisley silk tie and cummerbund; no one at Slater had seen anything so sharp. I was hugely impressed with him, so proud he was my date."

"Yeah, Ty's got cool clothes. He'd look cool in anything, though."

"Well, we'll have to get you a dress. I bet we could find something pretty at Nyheim's." She catches my wrist and holds it. "Sound good?"

"Mom, if we need the money—"

"Don't be a goon. This is important."

The waitress comes over and fills Mom's and my coffee cups. I open my mouth. Just ask her about the Greenhouse, I think. Now. Do it, do it. I've put this off for almost a week. I'm going to tell her I know where she was last night, and I'm going to ask her what the deal is, keeping this stupid secret from me. What comes out of my mouth is, "How was rehearsal last night?"

"Oh, Louis is having his last-minute panic attacks, of course." Mom shakes her head and grins like she's thinking back on something funny that happened.

Every day, the not-tell that has sprung up between us gathers a strange shape, growing thicker and more resistant to the truth.

The weekend blows by and Mom still won't tell me about her job, and since she's always out when I'm home and vice versa, I never find the right opportunity to talk with her. Everyone at Bradshaw knows she's working at the Greenhouse, though, mostly because Esther Zeller, a junior I don't know very well, buses tables there on weekends.

"Your Mom and I made a killing at the restaurant, Danny," Esther shouts and gives me a wink Monday afternoon, as I'm leaving the locker room. "You should've seen us move." A cluster of girls stand nearby, but no one speaks or looks at me, yet I sense a shifting, a quieting down of the noise level. They think I'm ashamed, I realize. Bunch of snobs. Then I think, Am I ashamed? And I know that I am, but part of the problem is that it's all mixed up with feeling angry and defensive and protective of Mom. Another part of the problem is that the person I want to talk with most about my feelings has decided not to talk to me about hers.

"It's not for a play, is it?" Portia asks later that same day.

"No, it's because Kahani's is closing down."

"We knew it." She snaps her fingers in my face. "That's what my dad had guessed, anyway. Look, you don't have to feel insecure about it with me, you know. Everyone totally loves your mom, Danny. We think she's so great, and everyone feels really bad that she's got to work that bummer job."

Really bad. Bummer job. Insecure. I hate feeling like Mom's and my finances are up for discussion. What goes on with people moneywise should be private, not discussed over mashed potatoes in the Paulsons' dining room or in the locker room at school. The whole situation feels like it's spinning way out of control. I write a note and stick it in the fridge.

Mom,
Please tell me what's going on with the Greenhouse. I don't know why you're feeling so private about it and I'd really like to talk to you.

Love, Danny

Just as I'm going to bed, though, I rip the note into confetti.

Late that night, I call the Greenhouse again, and listen to Mom shout, "Hello hello, who the hell is this?" I stare at the receiver and hang up.

On Tuesday, I make a very dumb fashion decision which, when I mull it over later, ends up adding a big fat worm to my unopened worm can. In a way it's my own stupid fault, but the boots had been hanging out in my closet for so long that their ugliness shock value was gone for me. So when I put them on Tuesday morning, while they didn't look stylish, they at least seemed like they were mine. Big mistake.

The curse of the ugly boots happened a couple years ago, when Mom and I went to a church rummage sale. Since we don't belong to any church, Mom was nervous, and she kept looking around like she thought the church sheriff was going to rush over any minute and kick us out.

"Mom, you don't have to be a member of a church to rummage here," I whispered.

"I'm not so sure about that, Danny," she said darkly. "But if they ask, say you belong to Saint Thomas." We couldn't find anything we liked, but Mom felt like she had to get something, so she impulsively bought a pair of cordovan, knee-high, cork-heeled, jangly, zip-up boots. Aside from being out of style, they were way too big for her, so she chucked them into my closet, where they remained, slouched against the back wall like two old drunks in the park. But whenever I've tried to throw the boots away, Mom makes me keep them. I swear she thinks it would be a sacrilege to throw away church-fair boots. She can be very superstitious like that.

Tuesdays are Bradshaw's weekly "casual day," which means, as long as you don't wear pants, you don't have to wear your uniform. I'm not a fan of shopping, and most Tuesdays I'll usually wear my uniform skirt with a sweatshirt on top. But this week, probably because Spring Fling is coming up, I'm thinking of different outfit possibilities for Saturday. So I dust off the boots and zip them up, pairing them with my short tan dress that doesn't match any of my other shoes.

"You need panty hose," Mom says, handing me a packet. "Otherwise, you look adorable." That should have been warning enough. But no bells go off in my head.

As soon as I walk into homeroom, Portia claps her hands over her cheeks and starts laughing. She runs over to me. "Eww, Danny. Those boots are just so, so icky, so *Welcome Back, Kotter.*" She sticks out her tongue at me. "Although I have to say—I admire your nerve."

"They're ironic," I say. "I wore them sort of as a joke." But then I double-check my locker just in case my basketball sneakers followed me to school. They didn't.

All morning, I feel girls' eyes staring down at my boots. To make matters worse, the panty hose almost immediately snag a run (I have no business wearing

Mom's size petite anyway). After lunch, I have a double free period, so I use it to go hide in the library until the end of the day. No one bothers me, and I'm almost home free until Hannah Wilder and Lacy Finn show up.

I can sense Hannah and Lacy's presence in the library before I actually see them. Hannah and Lacy know how to make other girls aware of them—not nervous, exactly—just very conscious that they're in the room. Maybe it's their clinky bracelets, or their barely stifled giggles, or the perfumy smell of their hair and book bags, but as soon as they walk through the library's double doors, I'm very aware of them.

"No, *you* shut up, you *loser*," Hannah hisses to Lacy.

"You're the loser," Lacy whispers back. Hannah and Lacy always crack themselves up, calling each other names like loser, since they and everyone else in the class know how cool they are. It makes me feel uncomfortable, because it gets me wondering who they think the *real* losers are.

I don't look up from the table until their minty breath practically curls into my face.

"Hey, Danny, doll face. Want one?" Lacy holds out a roll of breath mints.

"Thanks. What are you guys up to?"

"We were shortcutting to go hang out in the upstairs lounge, then we saw you and thought we'd say hi."

"Hi."

"You're going to the Fling with my cousin." Hannah slides up on the table and crosses her legs Indian style, yanking her miniskirt down between them to cover her underwear. "I talked to him last night."

"So, what're you wearing?" Lacy asks abruptly.

"I haven't thought about it. What're you guys wearing?" I counter.

"Je ne sais pas," Hannah says in a dumb-sounding southern drawl, rolling through all her vowels. "That's me being Dr. Sonenshine," she says, laughing. It's just the kind of Hannah joke I don't like, but I smile. Hannah has a way of making you join in on unfunny jokes.

"I don't know what I'm wearing," Lacy says, and then she looks at me in a friendly, thoughtful way. She rubs a finger over her chin. "But I bet you and I are about the same size. Hey, you know what, Danny?" She leans against the table and tilts her head as she studies me. "If you want, you can come over sometime tomorrow and look through my stuff. Most of my semiformal dresses I've only worn once; you know how my mom's such a shopoholic. Maybe you could borrow?"

"My mom's taking me shopping," I tell her. My voice feels glue thick. A setup. They've been talking about me, maybe even to Ty. About how I might not have the right dress for the Spring Fling.

"Too bad Portia's so teeny-tiny," Hannah says with a little giggle. "She has great clothes."

"Portia doesn't need to lend me an outfit. My mom and I are going shopping. For something new," I explain.

"If she has time, though. Doesn't she work a lot now, like, I know she has that new waitressing job?" Lacy doesn't wait for me to answer; she just plows ahead and I recognize a script when I hear it. "Hey, I might have an idea. My mom has credit over at Pagniti Marcello, since she returned all her birthday gifts. I know!" Lacy squeals and seizes my wrist. "We'll all go pick out something together: you, me, Mom, and Wilder." She smiles at Hannah. "And we'll get lunch at the club after. It'll be fun!"

My mind is reeling, planning my next move. If I get up from this table and walk out the door, I think, that gives them more than ten seconds of looking at my stupid zip boots and runny stockings. But if I keep sitting here, my face will just get redder, and worse, I might cry.

"You guys are really nice," I say carefully. "But my mom would be kind of disappointed if she thought I'd rather wear someone's hand-me-down than something new she wants to buy me."

"Oh my god, Danny, we are totally not saying that it's charity." Hannah's pretend worried face is enough to make me want to slap her.

"I'm going shopping with my mom, okay?"

"Did she help you pick out those boots?" Hannah says it light enough so that maybe, if you paid a fancy lawyer enough money, he could argue that it was meant only as kidding, but that's when I feel the tears behind my eyes.

"Oh, uh, no," I say with a laugh. "I actually got these at a thrift shop up in New York, in Manhattan." I stand up and look down at them, like I just at that moment noticed how awful they were. "Anyhow, I'm late for my math tutorial. I'll see you guys later."

I walk out of the library, my huge boot zippers jangling with every step, but I'm careful not to slam the door so they don't know how much they've upset me.

Once I'm safely in the faculty bathroom (which you

can lock), splashing water on my face and rubbing my hands over my chest splotches to calm them down, I let the tears come. The crying feels good, as if all of my doubts and problems, like these stupid boots, and Mom's job, and whether I'm going to find the right dress to wear to Fling, and wondering if Ty's going to call me tonight, and my crummy math grades, are all just rolling out of me, collecting into a big river of sludge.

I try for a smile, to reassure myself. The person in the mirror smiles back at me, but not with the carefree Rick Finzimer smile or the dead-on, ready-to-fight eyes of my mom. The girl in the mirror doesn't seem to be much of anyone, except a gigantic mess with a blotchy chest and puffy eyes and a pair of hideous boots on her feet.

CHAPTER

6

SHE HAD TO DESTROY something, anything. She thought of scissors, but a search through the house turned up only a tarnished silver butter knife. Nothing would stop her; she gripped handfuls of her shiny, waist-length hair and sawed at it until raggedy shanks of cerise lay in a heap on the bathroom floor, and jagged wisps fluffed out just above her ear. Her cats, Raison and Sprite, watched in fear, but her madness didn't end there. She ran to her mother's room and in a few minutes had shredded all her clothes to tatters, including her ugly cordovan zip skirt.

"Finally, I'm free," she whispered, clutching the knife in the air. Yet she could not quench this unbidden longing to slice, slash, and destroy. Suddenly the doorknob turned. Her father had come home! The knife sweat in her hand.

The Lilac contest rules had been to write "a dynamic first page to anything: novel, short story, fantasy, or science fiction text—you be the judge. Let your creative juices flow!" I didn't like the sound of the phrase "creative juices"; it made me think of my brain like a grapefruit, painstakingly squeezing out a sour trickle of pulp and seeds. But first place was a thousand dollars, then a five-hundred-dollar second place, and three more prizes of a hundred dollars apiece. And best of all—no entry fee.

"Hey, Danny, you want to come with me to rehearsal?" Mom calls.

"Why would I do that?" I shout, proofreading through my paragraph. I'm wondering about that word *cerise*. I don't think I know exactly what that word means.

"To run lines in the car? We could pick up Chinese, and you could see the dress rehearsal."

There's only an open can of tuna, an empty pizza box, and some of Gary's leftover Caesar salad in the fridge. It figures I'd have to be roped into watching Mom's stupid rehearsal just to get some dinner.

"Okay, hang on a minute while I get my jacket."

I close up my laptop and unfurl my cramped bones from the wobbling tortoiseshell, stepping out of it carefully.

Mom's on the phone, placing our order with Hunan Garden and snapping a raincoat over her Rosalind costume, which trails behind her in yards of worn brown velvet. A faded coronet of flowers is perched on top of her head.

"You look crazy," I tell her, frowning.

"Shakespeare would have appreciated raincoats. Stratford-upon-Avon probably got its share of downpours, don't you think?" She looks up at me and smiles.

"No comment," I say.

Neither of us takes umbrellas, and Mom's laughing as we dash out to the car. Her good mood makes my bad one worse. Old Yeller hacks and heaves a while before he hits his warming-up stage.

"Old Yeller's going in for inspection next week." Mom pats the dashboard. "Come on, baby. There's a boy. There's a boy. Ten minutes, buddy, you can do it."

"It's too dark to read this script." I squint at the chains of words.

"Never mind, lord help me if I'm not off-book by now . . . Danny, does this car smell funny to you? Like gas?"

I sniff. "I can't tell." We drive in silence a while, sniffing and frowning at each other. I jump out at Hunan Garden while Mom drives the car around the block because she doesn't know how to parallel park. Usually I don't care about Mom's bad driving but tonight, standing in the rain with soggy Chinese food bags and watching Old Yeller stalled at the red light across the street, I feel a burst of annoyance at her.

"Is the defroster on?" I ask when I get in.

The windshield wipers are chasing each other back and forth and don't do much to rub away the fog that films the glass.

"Broken." Mom sighs. "Okay, I smell something for real."

"All I smell is your gross cabbage cashew whatever-it-is that you ordered. You should really get this stupid car into the shop tomorrow."

"Why are being you such a sulky teenager lately?" Mom hunches over the steering wheel and squints out at the black road. "By the way—huge turnout for Tom Sawyer auditions. I think the girls really see this as a chance for fun for a change. People can let theater get so pretentious and affected, such a draw for world-class jackasses like Lemmon. Now this show—oh my gosh, Danny, did you feel that?"

"I didn't feel any—"

Old Yeller suddenly gives a shudder and a sad-sounding *brrrummmph*. I grip the sides of my seat as we reel forward.

"This is the end!" Mom shouts with the kind of expression that would make Louis proud. With a final hacking cough and a violent tremble, Old Yeller's tired old engine dies, right in the middle of Route 29.

"Please don't do this, you creep," Mom whispers, and for a second I think she's talking to me. She turns the key and presses her boot to the gas, then stomps on the gas, and the turning and stomping find a desperate rhythm. The angry bleat of car horns begins to sound all around us.

"I'll get out," I offer, opening the car door, "and I'll push." I saw that once in the movies, only it was a big brawny guy who did the pushing. But Mom looks at me with eyes full of thanks and hope, and I relent slightly in my bad mood toward her.

Being out in the middle of a highway on a rainy March night is something I've never experienced until tonight. Cars spin past me in a hiss of tires on water. Drizzly yellow highway lights send up oily reflections from the water-slicked road. I just hope the color of Old Canned Peas is bright enough to keep a car from hitting me.

I crouch and shove my body against the back of Old Yeller, pushing with each muscle that lets itself be pushed. Mom signals for me to hold on and then she gets out, too. She pushes the car from the driver side, reaching one of her hands inside to turn the steering wheel left. Slowly, painstakingly, we roll Old Yeller onto the shoulder of the road, to safety.

"We did it." Mom huffs and smiles at me through the dark downpour.

"Yeah, but now what?"

"I need to find a pay phone." Mom stands on tiptoe and peers ineffectively through the dark. "But it's a hike to that Aamco station. Almost a mile."

The car seems to have cruised straight out of nowhere; all at once a rain-glittering white Saab has pulled up right at our side.

"You need help?" A sheet of wet window glass rolls down and then I'm peering into the perfectly made-up face of Mrs. Finn. Mr. Finn is driving and, thankfully, there's no one in the back.

"Elizabeth, it's good to see you. Our car broke down." The words in Mom's mouth shake out a little too brightly. She sounds like she's acting at being someone else. I shoot her a warning look; *Masterpiece Theater* isn't the best idea right now.

"Get in, both of you. Hurry." There's a *cha-kunk*

sound of the automatic locks releasing and then Mom opens the passenger-side door. We slide inside the velvety leather of the Saab's tan interior and roll away from Old Yeller's broken body.

"Lucky thing we came along," Mrs. Finn says, waiting for us to thank her and agree.

"Thank you so much; it sure is lucky," Mom answers.

"Yeah, this is great," I add, although there are about a million names I would have put ahead of the Finns on my list of people I'd most like to be rescued by.

"I'll call the tow service." Mr. Finn nods, more to his wife than Mom, although his eyes dart at us from the rearview mirror. He picks up the car phone from the twinkling lights of his high-tech dashboard and starts punching up numbers.

"Now, where can we take you?" Mrs. Finn peers around at us from the front. Mom's coronet is half sliding over her eye.

"Oh, Bellmont People's Theater," Mom says happily. "I can't think what could have happened to that silly old car. I was planning to get it serviced last week, but one thing and another, you know how it goes!" She clasps her hands over her knees and laughs.

Mrs. Finn laughs, too, but there's a mean snicker

wrapped inside it. Mom just laughs harder, and with one hand I reach over and snatch off her flower wreath.

"You in another play, Susan? Bob and I just loved you in *The Little Foxes*. Susan's just adorable, I remember us saying. And we get such a kick out of those Kahani's commercials—'Right off Route 29.' And that's where we found you! Ha-ha-ha!" Mrs. Finn's laugh grates in my ears.

"It surely is nice of you, I must say." Mom smiles. I think I detect a southern accent.

I'm flashing to half an hour ahead in time, my mind's eye picturing Mrs. Finn bursting into the front door of her house, shouting, "Eeek, Lacy! You will never in a million years guess what we picked up on the side of the road!" I make myself squash away the image for now, and I turn to fix a permanent deadeye on Mom, as a hex to keep away her southern accent. After we listen to Mr. Finn deal with the car-towing people, the ten-minute drive passes in awkward silence.

"You all've been so terribly kind, rescuing Danny and me," Mom says, sweet as a mint julep, as we're getting out of the car in front of the Bellmont theater. I give her a little shove to keep her going.

"No problem." Mr. Finn hands her a card with the names and numbers of the tow place and garage that are handling Old Yeller. "Just let me know if there's anything else we can do for you."

"That was way beyond terrible," I say, stomping toward the front lobby of theater.

"You think?" Mom looks puzzled. "I'd call it a splash of Irish luck."

Mom always claims the nationality that suits her mood. I splash through every puddle. Mom dashes in front of me and yanks open the heavy glass doors of the theater. She unpeels her raincoat in a rush and makes a half-attempt to hold the door for me. She doesn't look back, and the door handle slips from my fingers, tearing my pinkie nail.

My anger has been brewing, and now it's at a full boil. I really want to start yelling. I want to ask Mom why she hasn't told me about the Greenhouse. I want to ask about why Rick Finzimer never calls and why she never let me toss those boots. I even want to yell at her about that time she decided it would be interesting to be Jewish and celebrate Passover with Louis and his wife, instead of having Easter. Even though it happened more than eight years ago, I still remember that the switch completely baffled me. I searched for jelly beans and eggs for days afterward.

Angry questions wiggle in my throat, caught against the smooth, strong current of Mom's lies. But I'm ready to fight.

The Bellmont People's Theater is an old stone building that used to be some founding Bellmont person's home. The lobby still has the look of a grand front entrance hall, with blown-up photos of past plays arranged like portraits on the walls. Mom's in a lot of them, wearing an array of costumes and wigs and different expressions.

There's even a Helen Keller and Annie Sullivan photo where I look kind of dazed (*a shockingly wooden performance . . .*) and a really great picture of Gary from the time Mom got him to be the butler in *The Importance of Being Earnest.* He looks sort of baffled, too, and I wonder if I can get a copy of the photo for him as a joke birthday gift.

Sometimes when I stand in the doorway and stare into the darkened empty theater, I understand why Mom loves being a Bellmont Player. All those rows of empty seats facing the stage are like hundreds of people silently holding their breath, waiting to listen to your elegant, perfectly prethought words, to watch your preplanned gestures, and to applaud your well-timed entrances and departures. It's a place where your story never goes wrong and always ends with people clapping.

You can get to the dressing rooms half a dozen different ways. I run, pretending I'm on the court, dribbling an imaginary ball down the middle aisle, leaping up onto the stage, which is set up for act 1, then faking out an imaginary Perry dork as I dance her up the apron, around the cardboard trees and behind the scrim until—slam dunk!—I soar high and smack my fingers on the top of the stage-right exit door, which leads to a long hall. The dressing rooms, bathrooms, and the green room, which is where the actors hang out and smoke cigarettes, all lead off from this hall, which I've seen painted two colors before its current shade of mushroom.

"Helen!" Joanne Field-Sterns greets me with a warm lipsticky kiss. She played my mother, Mrs. Keller, during my moment of Bellmont infamy.

"Hi, Joanne. Who are you?"

"Audrey, the shameless country wench." She flips her skirts. "Do I look slatternly?" She pushes up her mouth and flutters her eyelashes like Marilyn Monroe. Coal gray age lines have been etched on her forehead and at the corners of her eyes. The lines look fake up close, but onstage they'll magically transform Joanne into an old lady.

"If you want to, I guess," I say, as she starts kicking up her skirts like a cancan dancer. Some of the Bellmont Players can get a little nutty on you. I push down the line of chairs and women, just in time to catch an earful of Mom replaying her version of Old Yeller's breakdown.

"And there we were for what seemed like hours, just sopping wet, and I tell you, I had no idea what I was going to do, and Danny's practically in tears—oh, Danny, I was just telling . . ." Mom looks up from the mirror, where she's drawing a heavy black crow's feather of eyebrow over her eye.

I wave to Laura Drinker, Patsy Tepta, and someone I don't know. Their faces, all in full pancake stage make-up, are odd goldfish colors of yellow and orange. The dressing room is overwarm, overcrowded, and overbright from the dozens of exposed lightbulbs framing the dressing-room mirrors.

"Mom, can I talk to you for a second?" I move

behind her, sharing the space in the mirror with her, and we look at ourselves and each other both at once. Mom arranges a smile on her face.

"Sure," she says, perky as a Kahani's ad. I feel the other women exchanging looks and they tactfully begin to sidle away from us, down toward the other end of the dressing room. I wait until they're all pretty much out of earshot.

"Okay, look," I begin quietly. "I need to talk with you about something, but it's really hard to just jump in the middle of what I want to say, because—"

"Please don't tell me it's a blue slip in math. Danny, you promised you were going to get extra help on Tuesdays."

"Actually, I wanted to talk about the Greenhouse and this job that you're conveniently not telling me about."

Done. It's out, and suddenly I feel like the words need a lot more space to float around in.

"So what about it?" she asks. She makes her mouth a little knot and her one penciled-in eyebrow pushes down hard over her eye like a black lightning bolt.

"Well." I shake back my hair in a purposeful, Portia way. "I don't understand why you've kept this a secret from me."

"No secret. I'm on for three lunch shifts and two dinners, and I'm going to permanently pick up Sunday brunch when I get good enough. Okay?"

"Give me a break; you were too keeping it a secret and the whole school knows. Even Portia knew before me."

"I only thought I'd have the job for a couple weeks, until I figured out something better."

"You sure couldn't have figured out anything worse."

"And what's that supposed to mean?" Mom's face, closed as a button, doesn't make it easy for me to think out my next words.

"Okay, all right. Here's the thing. Why're you being a waitress when there's so many other—I'm not saying much better—but other jobs? Like if you were a receptionist or a salesperson in a clothes store like Gemma Bench's mom, or a, even a dental hygienist maybe. I mean, you're *serving* people, any old people, who could just walk in there. Like, like, Mr. Sallese. Or Portia. Just anyone. The Finns, even."

I breathe hard. Even the ceiling seems to pin us down into the strain of this moment. It's like the worms wiggled out of their can and sprouted from my hair, Medusa style. I take a step backward, trying to air out the damage. It's an ugly feeling, spitting out my darkest inside thoughts, especially when I see in Mom's reaction a face I only sometimes catch a glimpse of underneath all the other faces she wears. It strikes me now how young Mom's face is, almost like a kid's face, so different from the other Bradshaw moms.

When she speaks, her eyes don't leave my reflection in the mirror.

"Danny, you listen very clearly so you don't miss any of my words. Because right now you and I, we need money now. Waitressing pays well over any amount of money I could make selling blouses or answering phones. The Greenhouse also lets me keep Bradshaw hours and if I have to quit Bradshaw, you have to quit, too. And then you can go to Foxwood High. Maybe that'd be fun for you, Danny; we'll go buy you a bulletproof vest, combat boots, pack a gun in your lunchbox—"

"Forget it," I mumble. "I just meant that it's kind of embarrassing."

I half hoped I'd spoken inside my head; a thought, like a whisper, meant only for me. But I'd said it out loud. And now Mom swivels in her chair and stares at me with an almost frightened smile on her face, a frozen, disbelieving smile like I knocked the words right out of her. She stares at me like I'm a stranger and all she knows about me is that she doesn't like me.

"I can't look at you right now," she finally says. "You go away, I can't look at you right now."

"Fine." I slam out of the dressing room.

Of course there's nowhere to go, but the last thing I want to do is listen to Mom onstage, reciting her lines and singing and making jokes with Louis.

"I can't look at you, either," I say to her pictures in the lobby. I sit in the lobby armchair and work on my homework, and then on impulse pull my laptop out of my book bag and type:

Dear Rick Finzimer (Dad):
You probably got that card I sent you and thought I was some kind of JAPHTA—that's what my friend Portia and I call eighth graders. It stands for Just Another PinHead TagAlong. But I promise I won't start asking you for money, or whatever you think my plan is, getting in touch with you. It's not as though I'm plotting to run away and live with you, either.
Anyhow, the other day I was riding the train and across the seat from me I saw this man who looked sort of the way I picture you. He wore this gray hat that kept sliding over his eyes, no matter how many times he pushed it

back. It got me wondering, watching him, if you think about me the way I think about you, like if sometimes a picture of me falls over your eyes that you keep having to push back. Because there's lots of times I have to push back your picture.

Sometimes when Mom and I are in an argument (for instance, right now we are, which is why it's on my mind) I wish I had someone else in my family, kind of a fallback person, you know what I mean? Sometimes a family of two people is difficult, because if you aren't both on the same side, then your side is made up of just you. Which can be a little lonely, especially if you're not in the mood to be with just yourself.

So, that's all. I promise this is my last letter. Except if I do something like get married or win the Nobel Prize (ha!), then I'd let you know. I think.

Sincerely,
Dandelion L. Finzimer

When I read back through the letter, I can't decide if the whole thing seems too personal. Maybe I should stick to subjects most people feel more comfortable with, like sports or the weather.

Louis gives us a lift home, and he and Mom keep up a steady flow of conversation, but I know from the way she doesn't look at me that mending the rift that separates us will take some time.

Later that night, I can't sleep. The water stain on my ceiling changes shape, from a horse kicking up its legs to a man with a ponytail holding a barbell. My eyes are dry in their sockets, and I have to turn my clock radio away from me so I won't keep noticing the minutes flip into each other. Finally, I slide out of bed and turn on the light in hopes that reading *The Odyssey* might do the trick. It's hard to sleep on my anger.

The Cyclops chapter turns out to be not too deadly dull, and then I proof one more time through my creative-juiced story entry. I print it out and in the corner of an envelope I write my address and name, Antonia de Ver White. It looks elegant and professional.

I also print a copy of my letter to Rick Finzimer before I can second-guess myself, and then I fold the letter and the contest entry into their envelopes and kiss them both for luck. My eyes finally get that good scratchy feeling, and my dreams are full of prizes and reconciliations.

CHAPTER

7

"YOU WANT TO HEAR A STORY about Susan?" Gary puffs. Corkscrew snarls of hair are stuck to his forehead, and sweat collects in the hollow of his neck.

"Gary, you're losing steam," I laugh, looking at him. Underneath my arms and knees it's still dry as chalk. "We're at the homestretch, anyway. Twenty more minutes."

The AIDS walkathon ended up seeing a pretty heavy turnout, probably because of the early taste of spring in the air. Pale sun shines from a cloud-fluffed sky, and the rowing shells skimming over the Schuylkill River move as lightly as two-, four-, and eight-legged mosquitoes. All around us, people are walking and laughing and talking, and everywhere is the squishy smell of stirred-up mud. We're just rounding the bend of Kelly Drive where the art museum curves up at our left. Gary and I were close to the front lines of walkers at the beginning, but now other people are passing us. Friday pants and strains impatiently at his leash.

"Sorry, boy," I tell him. "I'd go faster, too; it's your old man who's keeping us back in the geriatric section."

"I need more B-12 vitamins," Gary huffs, trying to pick up speed. "Maybe more calcium."

"Tell me. Tell me your story about Mom." I feel like I've been talking too long anyway, finally dumping out all my problems of Mom and the Greenhouse and Hannah and smirking Mrs. Finn in a junk pile at Gary's feet. He's easy to talk to, though, because he never wastes time inflicting me with useless, out-of-touch adult advice. Gary just listens and then tells me funny stories to make me forget my problems.

"I'll tell you if you slow down for a minute. Must have been about ten, twelve years ago, when you were still little," Gary starts, and then he smiles at me, and I know he's remembering some dopey thing about how cute I was when I was little. I ignore his smile and stare ahead.

"Yeah?"

"Well, Susie was going to Hair Express to get her coloring done by this character, I'll never forget her name. Fiona. Fiona'd given Susie a whole spiel of how she was working twenty million jobs, saving money to send her boyfriend to night school, and how she lived in a little row house with about eighteen sisters and a sick dog, ek setra, ek setra. Your basic extreme hard-luck case, I forget all the details. But Fiona's constantly doing a terrible job on Susie's hair. Ugh, she looked like— remember Tina Turner's hair in *Mad Max 3: Beyond Thunderdome?* Like that. And this was before Susie went red, you know, she was a peroxide blond. So you need a pro for those kinds of chemicals."

"Gary, is this story on the right track to an ending?"

"Pipe down there, Wombat." Gary teases a snarl out of the Walkman cord hooked around his neck. "Unless you want me to turn on my music instead."

"I'm listening, I'm listening."

"So Susie's in there, bonding with Fiona, listening to her gripe, while at the same time Fiona's just *butchering* Susie's hair: parts yellow, parts white, parts still that nectarine color when the dye doesn't pick up. And Susie'd been trying for weeks to think of a way to tell Fiona that she was switching to A Cut Above, but finally she just blurts out, 'I hate to tell you this, Fiona, but today's the last time I can come here because my company's moving me to Israel.'"

"Israel?" I snort. "Why'd she say that?"

"She said it was just the first thing that popped into her head; Bellmont was doing *Jesus Christ Superstar,* and her mind was sort of thinking down that line. But, so, Fiona goes, 'Well, I guess I won't be seeing you around anymore,' ek setra, and—"

"Et cet-er-a," I say. "It's Latin. It means, 'and the rest'—"

"Hey, Breedshow princess. Do you want to hear the end of this story?"

"Yes, sorry. Keep going."

"So Susie was so paranoid that Fiona would find out that all she did was change hairdressers, not countries, that Susie actually bought some sunglasses and a wig. She kept them in her pocketbook for over a year. We'd be out shopping or something, and Susie'd get these phantom Fiona sightings and start going, 'Gary, Gary, help me put on my wig!' And it'd be on all crooked with her real hair falling out. She was out of her mind at the idea Fiona'd know she was still in Foxwood. She also took all these long ways around town so she'd never get in the vicinity of Hair Express."

"Hey, Aesop, is there a moral here?"

"Not really," Gary huffs. "Except that Susie's a little bit batty. Let's pick up some speed now. I'm feeling strong. Maybe after, we can race up and down the steps of the art museum."

When I think about it later that afternoon, though, I see why Gary picked that story. Mom tends to create a lot of trouble for herself when all she wants to do is to get out of a little trouble. And once she's convinced herself of a plan, she has a tough time abandoning it. It'd be hard to know how long Mom thought she could hide her job from me; if I hadn't said anything, she might have held me off for months.

Now we're in a not-speak, a stalemate that I don't think either of us knows how to break. I even took the earlier train in yesterday morning so I didn't have to talk to her. It depressed me; usually when Old Yeller's in the shop and Mom and I have to take the train, we'll get breakfast together at the Stationhouse Café, splitting the pancake-and-eggs special. Yesterday I just got a corn muffin.

I know I should apologize, and I want to, but underneath my apology feelings hide thick wrinkles of resentment. Why should I be the one to go to her, when she was the one who kept her secret from me in the first place?

She spends most of the weekend in rehearsal and so

her refrigerator messages to me are brief, without my name, without "XO's" or "Love, Mom's."

> Please write a check for the exterminator.
> Remember to put the towels in the dryer.
> We need bagels.

Cold as the tone of the notes is, for some reason I can't toss them in the garbage can as usual. I put them in the silverware drawer instead.

As I'm heading out the door for school Monday morning, though, I see a note on the table that reads:

> For the dance.

Next to the note is a blank check made out to Nyheim's. I guiltily crumple the check into my pocket. After school, Portia and I go to Nyheim's and I get a yellow dress on sale that Portia swears makes me look like Princess Di but I think makes my skin look jaundiced. Still, I know better than to stand in the way of Portia's fashion authority.

That evening, I spread the dress over the back of the couch and leave her a note.

> Thanks, Mom.

I know she sees the dress and the note when she gets

back from her shift that night, but she doesn't come into my room. She walks past my closed door and then shuts the door to her room. The apartment seems emptier at that moment than it ever does when I'm here by myself.

A chunk of reality can be as tricky to catch as it is to throw, especially if someone's throwing while you aren't looking. When Ty Amblin called to cancel our date the night before the Spring Fling, the hurt of it caught me off guard. The reason Ty gave was this:

"The problem is, my aunt just had a baby and she and my uncle are going to be staying with us this weekend, and my mom's having a fit that we're all home for family stuff. Big dinner, you know the drill."

"Yeah, that's too bad," I say. My scalp and neck jolt with shock prickles. What a pathetic excuse. All I want is to get off the phone. "Can you hang on a second?" I ask. I cover the receiver with my hand. "Coming, I'm coming!" I yell through the empty apartment. "My mom's calling," I explain. "I better go."

"Sorry about this whole thing," Ty says. "I hope it doesn't rot too much."

"Well. I guess not too much. So . . ." I pause, wanting

to hang up and half hoping that he'll save me by suggesting something else, another plan, anything. But the line goes quiet, and then I feel even more stupid and desperate. "Talk to you later," I say quickly.

"Yep," he practically carols.

I stare at the phone for a long time after hanging up, chewing my nails. Then I grab the receiver and press speed dial number three.

"You're kidding," Portia says. "Oh my God, what a creep. I'm going to cancel on Jess."

"Don't," I say. "That'd only be dumb." We fall into silence, just sitting together over the wire.

"Portia, do you think he bagged out because I'm? . . ." It's hard to come out and say it. I try to go around another way. "Is there anything you know about Ty, anything that would make you think he might not want to hang out with me because of, I don't know, like living out in Foxwood or, you know how I told you about that thing with Lacy and Hannah in the library, or Mom's job—anything like that?"

"I don't know, but Ty Amblin's a jerk and a snob and I totally hate him," Portia says, and her words pounce on Ty so quick and mean that they make me feel more certain that my instincts are right. Portia probably feels weird telling me. "Those cheesy golf sweaters?" she says instead. "And I saw him at the club the other day and he was wearing these pants with a little squash racquet design on them. I mean, one thing if it's a belt, but pants? He should go ahead and date that worm-face Hannah, didn't people marry their cousins in olden days?"

"Yeah, and then all their kids would have that disease."

"Hemophilia," Portia says. "Isn't that it? Ty definitely did not belong with you."

"Definitely not." And then I have to spend about ten minutes convincing Portia that it's okay for her to go to the dance without me.

"But I'm not going to have any fun," she insists.

After hanging up, I plop a pillow inside my tortoise-shell and roll into a ball, just listening to myself breathe in and out, long trembly breaths, while the sunlight slips out of my room. My mind is jumping everywhere at once, spinning me around with questions I don't know how to answer. Is there anyone else I could take? (No.) Do I even want to go at all? (Not really.) Did Hannah tell Ty about my zipper boots? (Probably.) Do I really want to sit around by myself on Saturday night? (No, but I bet I will.) The only reason I wanted to go to the Fling was because of Ty. I don't want to go alone, and I don't want Portia figuring out some kind of awful last-minute setup.

I picture Mom and Rick Finzimer, dancing together at her spring formal. He wears a flashy tie and she's dressed in my yellow dress from Nyheim's. Was Rick Finzimer ever ashamed of Mom? Were his nails soft and polished like Ty Amblin's? I bet my nails grossed Ty out. I bet he never really wanted to go to the dance with me. He just knew that I liked him and would have gone with anybody, until Lacy and Hannah informed him that showing up with me would be worse than showing up with a giant jaundiced yellow cockroach.

I drag myself into the living room to watch TV while painting my nails with some gluey red nail polish I discovered under the couch. I try to stop the sad feelings from squirming into my heart, which I picture in the shape of one of the decoration flowers we tacked up in the gym for the Fling: pink and flat and papery, easy to scrunch.

When Mom comes home I feel too stupid to tell her about Ty, plus then I'd have to apologize for our fight, even though I wouldn't call it a fight exactly, anymore. It's more of that unsure, niggly stage right before a truce. So I stay in my room. But she decides to make dinner and then I have to sit at the table and eat an evil plateful of tuna fish sandwiches and cauliflower. I chew and swallow in silence. Mom reads a magazine. I clean up the kitchen without being asked. The quietness in the apartment hurts almost as much as the imaginary brawling conversations I'm having with Ty Amblin in my brain.

Saturday is opening night for *As You Like It.*

"Have a good time at the dance," Mom says as she heads out the door. Her voice isn't friendly or mean; I could answer nicely or not at all. She really knows how to deliver her lines perfectly; there's no substitute for that kind of talent. I decide to answer seminicely.

"Okay, I will."

"And are you staying over at Portia's?"

"I guess so." It takes every nonbabyish, unselfish feeling inside me to keep from running to the door, stopping her, and pouring out my problems. I really don't want to be by myself tonight, which now stretches before me in all its miserable, agonizing hours of lying around, flipping through magazines or TV channels, thinking about the dance. "Break a leg tonight," I add after a second's thought.

"Thanks." She smiles, a real smile that might mean

we're on the road to patching things up. But then she opens and walks out the door, locking the deadbolt with a purposeful, leaden clunk that makes me feel like a prisoner. Now I am officially trapped inside my horrible Saturday night.

The phone rings and some cruelly optimistic voice inside me convinces me that it's Ty. Would I still go to the dance with him, even last minute? No. Yes. No.

I pick up the phone and take a breath.

"Hello?"

"Hi."

"Oh. Hey, Gary."

"I just made a beautiful chef's salad," he says. "And I thought I could bring you a Breedshow princess-size portion, to give you enough energy for the ball."

"Oh, Gary, that's so nice of you," I say. "But I'm not . . . it's just one of those, see I'm not exactly . . . see Gar, it's a long story." I am trying very hard not to sound too pathetic, but I guess I must, because the next thing I know Gary is at the door, holding a bowl of chef's salad in one hand and half a loaf of his awful health-food-store, honey-sweetened walnut bread in the other.

"I'm in the mood for a long story," he says, "as long as you have forks."

The truth is that it's not a long story at all. It's a short angry one. I don't bother to act like Miss Cool when I tell it, like I sort of did with Portia. Gary knows me too well. And then, I don't know why—mostly I think it's just because I'm not ready to stop crying yet—but I start talking to him all about Rick Finzimer, and how he manages to crawl his way inside my thoughts more than I'd like him to, these days.

"I can't help wishing I could pick up the phone and talk to him every once in while," I say. As soon as I've said it out loud, I know it's true. "Like if I ever get a not horrible grade in math, or when I didn't know whether to get Mom those earrings for her birthday. I guess I want to share life stuff with him. A good time or a bad time, or anything."

"You know, Wombat, I hope you always know you can rely on me to talk to and do some of that parent duty."

"Oh, I know," I say quickly. I don't mean to hurt Gary's feelings. "It's more that I wish Rick Finzimer cared in the first place. And it's not like I'm constantly moping about him; I mean, the fact that I miss him at all kind of surprises me."

"I hear you," Gary says. He turns his attention to the

bread, cutting a small slice for himself and a huge chunk for me. "Some days when I'm at work, and I'll be having a good day, kind of involved in it, kind of distracted, that's when Elliot hits me. Just like— gotcha." He snaps his fingers. "It's this split moment of 'Hang on—why isn't this day as good as I think?' And at the same time, I'm swamped by my remembering, by a, I don't know, maybe a drowning feeling, like a realization of 'Oh, yeah, that's right, Elliot's dead, remember? Remember how the person you loved more than anyone in the world is gone for good?' "

I don't know if Gary means to say this last sentence out loud and for a moment we have to sit back from it. Then he laughs and shakes his head a little as if to shake off his thoughts.

"I doubt if I can finish this monster slab of walnut bread," I say, to lighten the mood.

"It's revolting," Gary agrees, rolling his eyes. "Don't bother."

"Well, if it's revolting, why do you keep buying it?" I ask.

"I have friends at the health food store," he says. "They were friends of Elliot's actually. They sucker me into buying all the food that's not selling."

"So this bread actually is Elliot's fault," I say with a smile.

"Hey, I guess it is." Gary nods. "Blame dessert on him."

"Thanks a lot, Elliot." I make a face. "This bread tastes like Styrofoam."

"Yep, thanks, Elliot," Gary says. "You and your legacy of tofu-chomping, tree-hugging friends." Gary waves his sliver of bread at the ceiling. We laugh together, which feels good after an evening of so many sad words.

Later that night I wake up to the sound of Mom's keys jingling softly in the lock. My clock says 3:12 A.M.; Mom must have gone to the cast party at Louis's house after. When I was little and Mom came home from shows, she'd always tap on my door and whisper, "Still awake?" and if I was (and I always was because my sleep-ears were trained to hear her voice thanking and paying the baby-sitter), I would jump out of my bed, into her room, and jump in her bed. Then she'd tell me about her night and I'd tell her about mine.

I wish I could ask her how opening night went, if Duke Senior missed his final cue, and if Laura cut Mom off in their "I pray thee, Rosalind, be merry" scene in act 1.

And I wish I could tell her about jerkhead Ty.
But tonight there's no tap.

The next morning I wake up early, ready for some kind of a truce. I run out to the 7-Eleven and buy honey-glazed doughnuts and two coffees and the paper and even a bunch of daisies, arranging everything on the coffee table in the living room, like it's a fancy hotel continental breakfast.

"You're great," Mom says, smiling and rubbing her eyes when she sees the table. Faint traces of eyeliner smudge down her cheeks. "But why aren't you at Portia's?"

"Ty canceled last minute. He turned out to be sort of creepy."

Mom's face holds no expression of pity or sadness or any of those things that make me feel more stupid than I do already. She just shakes her head and bites into her doughnut, then she says, "There was this show I did once where someone, I think it was the gruff grandfather character, said, 'Some people don't split right when you cut them open.' I can't remember the play but I never forgot that line."

"Yeah, that's kind of how he was."

"But you must be depressed," Mom says carefully.

"I am," I answer. "I just don't feel like talking about it right now." I'm glad I already poured everything out on Gary instead of Mom. Sometimes Gary makes a good fallback person.

We drink coffee and read the paper and life feels back to seminormal again. After a while, I stand up to go to my room, deciding finally to start my *Odyssey* paper, when there's a soft knock on the door.

"Who's that?"

"Will you get that, it's probably Gary," Mom says. "He said he might come by to borrow our waffle maker."

Expecting Gary but then seeing another face is like taking a sip of milk and finding out it's really lemonade; it's the sheer surprise that scares you most. I catch my breath in a scream and jump back like a spooked cat when I see the strange man lurking in our doorway. It only takes me a second to recognize him, which answers a question I'd asked myself my whole life: Would I instantly know my father if I saw him?

Tall. That's the second thing I think. Rick Finzimer is really tall and rangy, like me. The third thing I think is that he looks scared.

CHAPTER

8

"Hi," I SAY IN A VOICE THAT gets swallowed up in my throat. Rick Finzimer's nervous gaze holds mine for a long second, and then his eyes find Mom. The stare and silence last a long time.

"I thought we'd made a deal," he says to her. "You and I." I move like a slow propeller, shifting to look over at Mom, who is sitting motionless. She's holding her paper coffee cup in midair. Her face is a replica of Annie Sullivan's expression at the end of the play, when she hears Helen say "wa-wa," and in her eyes you see all the disbelief and shock and feverish excitement of something incredible coming true.

"Richard," she says. She touches her fingers to her temples and her hair, and her eyes grow into two Os that take over her entire face.

Meanwhile, all I can do is soak in all this dumb information: how Rick Finzimer's soft tassel shoes are the same kind as Mr. Paulson's, how he has reddish blond hair that sprouts from a bed of freckles on his wrists and hands, that he's wearing a sharp cologne I recognize as Bay Rum, because Louis wears too much of it, too.

"Richard, you could knock me down with a feather," Mom finally says. "I can't believe it's you."

"It's me," he says quietly. He can't tear his gaze away from her.

"Richard." Mom lifts her chin and clears her throat. "Richard, this is your daughter." She springs up from the sofa and in a second has whisked next to me, her hand on my shoulder, and I want to tear off her smile, because it's so big and proud and I don't see how I can live up to it right now. "Our daughter, Dandelion."

"Danny," I correct. I am breathless with the horror of this situation. I want to slam the front door right now and run into the bathroom and take a shower and brush my hair and even then maybe not come out for a little while. Not until I'm ready. I can't believe this is happening now. Meeting Rick Finzimer absolutely should not be happening now, when I haven't practiced for it.

"Well, Danny," he says. "I got your letter."

"Both of them?" I ask. He looks baffled for a second, then he nods.

"But you know which one I'm talking about."

"You've been writing to each other?" Mom's voice is tiny, a doll voice.

"*I* have." I feel warmly uncomfortable; my hand reaches automatically to close up the top button of my shirt. "Just a couple letters. I got the address from the phone book, sort of. I called up my uh. Your, um . . . "

"My parents," Rick Finzimer says. "That's what I assumed." He shoves his hands in the pockets of his dark green corduroys. Ty Amblin–style pants, I can't help thinking.

Something is wrong, though. His eyes are so hard and thoughtful on me, like I'm a criminal he's trying to identify in a lineup. "I guess I have to believe, Susan, that you didn't okay this."

"No," Mom says. "No, we'd made a deal, I never broke that deal. But I can't monitor—"

"It was just a stupid letter." I hear the squeakiness in my words but I can't stop myself. "It wasn't supposed to make you mad or anything. You didn't have to come here all the way from California—"

"You live in California?" Mom asks wonderingly.

"Los Angeles." Rick Finzimer nods. "But I'm in Philadelphia on business right now. I should have called first, maybe. This is actually a bit spontaneous for me, but ah . . . " He reaches into his pocket and pulls out a sheet of typed paper, which he waves at Mom. "I thought I ought to come by in person to talk about this—death threat? Is that what this is, Danny? Are you threatening me?" His tone isn't unkind, but the sense of his words confuses me and his expression is careful, a composed blank.

"What are you talking about?" I ask. I am genuinely stumped. Is he playing some kind of joke? Rick Finzimer's face shows no glimpse of amusement.

"A death threat?" Mom breathes. "I don't believe it."

"It's right here." He hands the paper over to her with raised-eyebrow assurance.

"Give me a break, there's no death threat in there." I grab at the paper, my long arms flailing, trying to think straight. Why is he doing this to me?

That's when my eyes pick out a sliver of sentence, "this unbidden longing to slice, slash, and destroy . . ." My paragraph, my entry for *The Lilac* contest. The realizing comes at me like a punch; I must have switched the entry with my Rick Finzimer letter, put them in the wrong envelopes by accident before I mailed them out.

And that stupid ending with the knife and the dad coming home must have seemed like I was threatening him. . . . The realization almost chokes me. I'm such a flake. How humiliating. I want to crawl underneath my tortoiseshell and die.

"Mom, it's not really a threat; it's one of my contests," I whisper close to her ear. Mom reads quickly, her eyes darting to me after she hits the last sentence. "A contest," I hiss. "For a story. I messed up the mailing."

"By the way, I'm allergic to cats, so I can't stay here long," Rick Finzimer says. He pulls out a handkerchief from his pocket.

"Cats?" Mom echoes. I have never seen her in command of so few words.

"Your cats, Raisin and Sprite."

"The story, it's—he thinks we have cats." I want to shake the shocked stare off Mom's face. I jab my finger at the paper. "Will you explain it to him? Please? I can't. I'm really really sorry. It's all a great big huge horrible mistake."

"A contest." Mom glances at the story again and then up at me.

"Please," I say. I swallow hard to steady my voice but all my words have dried up. Without another look at Rick Finzimer, I fly out of the room, down the hall to my bedroom, where I slam the door.

I lie on the bed and squeeze my eyes shut, willing

myself not to be in this apartment, in this situation. Mom's understanding of what happened must finally kick in, because through my closed door I can tell she has on her reasonable voice. I listen to the muffled but steady hush of her explanation and then this other voice, this unfamiliar male voice that isn't Louis's or Gary's or Elliot's, but actually is the voice of my own flesh-and-blood dad. This isn't how my imagination had ever thought up the day I'd meet my father. This day is too stupid and awkward and full of speechlessness. I press my pillow over my head, turning my world soft and dark.

About half an hour later I hear the front door open and then quietly shut. I listen to Mom padding down the hall and then her fingers tapping on my door.

"Come in."

"Danny, are you crying?" Mom sits on the edge of the bed and pulls off the pillow. She peers into my face for clues.

"No."

"He's gone now."

"Good."

"But he wants to take you out to breakfast tomorrow, and he invited us both for lunch tomorrow afternoon at his parents' house. He felt sorry about the whole . . .

misunderstanding, with the letter. And he's going to talk to his parents now, tell them about you, and us, and then tomorrow, if it's okay, we can go meet them. I'll let you skip school, since it's a special occasion. Only if you want to." Mom's voice is soothing, like when I'm sick with the flu. "So, maybe it was a good thing, your writing this letter. It's sort of funny, too, when you think about it. Maybe something like this should have happened long ago."

I raise myself up so I'm slouching against the headboard.

"What do you mean, tell his parents about us?" I ask. "They don't know about their own granddaughter?"

"Okay, Danny, here's the thing."

"They never knew about me? But what you said, you said it was a really ugly falling out and that they had a spiteful grudge against us, you said . . . " I try to sort and file through Mom's story.

"I said some things and I didn't say some other things. But if you want me to tell you the other things now, I will. I'm ready."

"Just tell it in a simple way, okay? The way it really happened, without all those—" I ripple my fingers in the air. Without all those made-up stories stuck in the cracks to hold the truth together. "Simple," I repeat. I close my eyes and try to calm my racing mind, waiting for the truth I hope she'll put there.

"Simple, all right. Your dad." Mom inhales and lets her breath out slowly, like she's doing one of her voice warm-up exercises. "I told you how I met him in Philadelphia in the spring of my senior year of high school. You know I worked in the cafeteria of the art museum on weekends for extra money, and your dad came in one day. It was just one of those things, Danny, when your eyes lock—"

"Skip those parts, please," I mumble. "I know those parts, about how he was so smart and great and how he took you to your first Broadway play and everything. Just tell me the facts."

"We were never married," Mom says.

There's a fact. I can't even move for a second from the thud of this fact dropping inside my stomach.

"Why not?"

You aren't even really Rick Finzimer's daughter, I'm saying to myself, except technically. So it doesn't matter, it doesn't matter. Who cares if they were married or not? But a sour taste fills my mouth (*uncertain whether to laugh or scream . . .*), and a terrible steam of anger rises off my skin. Anger against Mom. "Why not?" I say louder.

"He didn't want to. No, that's not fair. Of course he didn't want to, he was eighteen, I was eighteen. Who gets married that young? He was leaving for college in Vermont that fall."

"You met him in the spring and he left for college in the fall?" How pathetic; I'm the result of something that was nothing. The soap-opera marriage Mom described probably came right off a real soap opera she was watching while she sat around being eighteen and pregnant and ditched by her summer-fling boyfriend.

"In the spring I wasn't thinking about the fall. See, Danny, where I came from, from Slater High School, from West Philly, you couldn't find someone as glamorous as Richard Finzimer anywhere. The way he talked, and he drove this little red car, and his clothes . . . he reminded me of a movie star. Rick was so different from anything I'd ever seen in real life."

"Just because of a nice car and nice clothes?"

"You're right, of course you're right. But you didn't grow up the way I did, hopping between families, living on the fringes. I didn't fit in anywhere. At the time, there was something about him, that look of really belonging somewhere."

"You had the Massaras." I shrug. "You belonged to

them, sort of."

"The Massaras were very supportive," Mom agrees. "They even said they'd take care of you, raise you, if I couldn't."

"Oh that would have been a good life for me. With all their crazy rules and sixty hours of prayers before dinner and their post-expiration-date food."

"They're good people, Danny." Mom catches my wrist and I shake off her grip.

"Well, they're probably not liars," I say. "At least I could have grown up in a house where people told me the truth every once in a while."

"I'm sorry, Danny." Mom stands up. "I did the best I could. And I'm sorry he wasn't any kind of dad to you, but the truth is he never wanted to be a father, and I never wanted you to feel . . . neglected, I guess. So I invented a few things."

"Like my bead necklace and my cassette player and my tortoiseshell? He never sent those things, did he? Was it you who gave those to me?"

"It was easier," Mom says. She stands up and starts walking toward the door. "And I did stop pretending, once you got older. I think that in some ways, too, I was pretending for both of us."

"You can't go yet," I tell her. "I have a million questions. You have to answer them all."

"My shift starts in fifteen minutes," Mom says softly. "Your million questions will have to wait a little while."

Later that night she answers more of my questions, with none of the answers I want. She's honest. She tells me about how Rick Finzimer tried to give her money for an abortion, how he begged her never ever to tell his parents about me, because he'd be in so much trouble. How he visited her only once just after I was born and even then pleaded with Mom to put me up for adoption. It's shocking to realize how much a person who didn't even know me didn't want me. But the truth feels like a long hot shower, a washing off of all those muddy, half-buried contradictions of Mom's stories and not-tells.

"Why did you have me then?" I finally ask.

"I wanted a family," she answers. "Something all my own."

Selfish, I think. Typical. Wanting something for herself, but she never stopped to think I might need something of my own, too. Like my own father.

Later that night, I throw that stupid broken cassette player right into the kitchen trash can, so that Mom is sure to see it the next morning.

CHAPTER

9

T H E R E ' S   A   P O R C H and rocking chairs, just as I'd imagined. It's a wraparound, with potted spider plants hanging from the latticework, and the two painted rocking chairs have little tie-back cushions. What I never could have guessed, though, was that there'd be cats. Dozens of glazed ceramic cats peek and prowl and lurk in every available corner.

"You like them?" asks Mrs. Finzimer. "I always wanted real ones, but Ricky being allergic and all, these were the next best thing. I mold and paint them myself. Keeps me busy." She's not at all what I expected; she's round and stubby as a pigeon with a pigeon's startled, unblinking eyes, and her gray hair is feathered close to her scalp like a boy's.

"Wow," I answer respectfully.

As soon as I walk in the front door the whiff of lemon air freshener that seems to sharpen the focus of the room makes me queasy. I want to turn around and run straight back to the car and hide. But I don't. I adjust Mom's scarf over my collar and chest, and allow a polite smile to hold up my mouth. What a day this is turning out to be.

Rick Finzimer arrived at 4M early this morning, true to his word, and took me out to breakfast. Mom acted more concerned about the breakfast than I did, getting up at six in the morning to iron my blue linen dress and polish my shoes before heading out to work the brunch shift at the Greenhouse.

"And wear your headband, to keep your bangs out of your face," she mentioned twice before she left. She even balanced the headband on top of my toothbrush so I'd be sure to see it.

The breakfast was tough. Luckily, though, Rick Finzimer did most of the talking. He told me how people who live in Europe are obsessed with American sportswear and that he had a good business going, selling baseball caps to department stores in Brussels and Madrid. I found out about his two boys, six-year-old Morgan and three-and-a-half-year-old Madison. I found out about his wife, Caren with a *C*, whom he met at graduate school in California. She's a strict vegetarian and can make tofu taste like chicken or beef or swordfish—Elliot probably would have loved to trade recipes with her. I found out that Rick Finzimer's doctor advised him always to live on the West Coast, because the thinner air helps his bad sinuses.

I found out all these things before ordering my eggs and juice. I also found out that I can sum up all the major points of my own life in under an hour, and still leave myself plenty of room to stretch out inside uncomfortable silences. We weren't able to have a good laugh over the letter mix-up, even after I apologized. He kept looking at me with the eyes of someone who's still on his guard, trying to figure out if I might be a psychopath. It was an uncomfortable feeling for us both.

"So you're interested in writing violent books?" he asked at one point.

"Not exactly," I answered. "I was just in a bad mood the day I wrote about the girl cutting off her hair."

"Do you consider yourself to have a bad temper?" he asked.

"Not really," I answered. The conversation never got much better than that, although we had a couple of good minutes talking about the 76ers' odds of making the NBA playoffs.

After breakfast I was full of stress and eggs Benedict, and my stomach wasn't having the greatest reaction to either. Rick Finzimer dropped me off at the apartment in his parents' sedan and said, "See ya in a few." I waved to him as he drove away and then crawled back into bed to sleep.

And now, here I am, breakfast barely digested, about to sit down to another strange meal that I don't really want to eat.

"Isn't this nice?" Mom asks nobody in particular as we stand in the hall. No trace of her suggests that a couple of hours before, she was carrying food trays and coffee pitchers, zooming all around the Greenhouse. Her hands are scrubbed pink and she's even wearing her best perfume, Zanzibar, which Louis's wife gave her six Christmases ago.

The Finzimers' furniture is all the color of hot-dog toppings. A mustardy rug stretches through the whole downstairs and a ketchup-and-relish pattern swirls through all the matching upholstered furniture. The house seems to be made mostly of dark corners, even in the family room, which is where Mrs. Finzimer leads us since "the light's better in here."

We sit: my mother, my father, my grandmother, and I.

"Big Rick's out in the woodshed," Mrs. Finzimer says as she plumps herself deep into a recliner. "He'll be along soon." There's a bag of knitting on the floor beside her; she reaches for a folded square of yellow before she thinks better of it and returns her hands to a little round ball in her lap. "I sure am sorry I couldn't have stolen some more time to prepare a nicer lunch; this was quite a shock for me, last night. I must say I had to think quite a while before I could even put a picture of you back into my head, Susan."

She smiles as she says this and I notice one of her front teeth is crooked. *My grandmother has a crooked front tooth.* I've been checking off these facts to myself the minute we pulled onto pleasant, tree-lined Poplar Avenue. *My grandparents' house is beige-colored stucco. My grandfather has a woodshed.*

"Well, I only visited here a few times," Mom says, patting wisps of her hair behind her ears and leaning forward in a gesture that to me seems a little bit over-friendly. "So it's only natural you wouldn't remember me."

"Oh, but I do." My grandmother nods. "It was in the summer. You were wearing a real tight miniskirt. I recall it, because it had a goldfish pattern, and because it was so tight. And your shoes with those real high—"

"Strange how I don't remember that outfit." Mom cuts her off with a smile. She gently bounces a shiny foil-wrapped present on her lap like a baby. "Teenagers sure can be goofy, though, huh?" This statement is met with silence from the room. "We brought you something," Mom continues chattily, addressing Mrs. Finzimer. I keep wishing she'd call her a name like Paula or Mrs. Finzimer, so I'd know what to call her, but I guess Mom doesn't know, either. "Just a silly little thing from Danny's and my favorite tea shop in town, isn't that right, Danny?" She half stands and passes the box to Mrs. Finzimer.

"Uh-huh," I say, almost under my breath. These pointless conversations have been squeezing themselves out painfully from the moment we arrived. I try harder, for Mom's sake. "More like a coffee shop."

"Oh, how nice." The crooked tooth appears again. "What do we have here?" She unwraps the ribbons and shiny paper, and her hands poke through the layers of tissue before pulling out six earthenware coffee mugs. "How nice," she repeats with the exact same inflection. "Really, you shouldn't have. They're very nice." She holds up a mug for Rick Finzimer to see and then she slides the box down next to her knitting.

"Just a nothing thing, really." Mom clears her throat. She crosses her legs and then crosses them the other way, smoothing a hand over the back of her skirt. It's surprising to me that Mom decided to dress pretty normally for the visit. I was expecting her army lug-sole boots or her good-luck-dragon beaded shawl—even her blond china-doll wig, if she was really feeling the need for disguise. But in her striped red shirt and silver necklace and with her hair combed flat into a braid behind her ears, she looks like she could have been anyone's mom.

"Do you drink a lot of coffee?" Mrs. Finzimer asks, glancing down at the mugs.

"Too much, I'm afraid." Mom laughs apologetically.

"It's very bad for you." Mrs. Finzimer holds up her hand and turns her face like she's refusing a cup right at that moment. "Caffeine."

"I never let Danny drink it," Mom says, pointedly avoiding my deadeye.

"It can stunt your growth," Mrs. Finzimer says, her pigeon eyes direct on me. I can't figure out if that's her way of telling me that I'm too tall and maybe should have enjoyed a little more caffeine when I had the chance.

"Danny's a basketball player," Rick Finzimer

mentions. He stares out the window as he says it, his eyes captivated by the empty street outside. "She's captain of the freshman team," he adds.

"She's the best player in the whole school," Mom says. I glare at her, but the years have taught me that Mom has no bragging censor.

As soon as she got back from her Greenhouse shift this morning, Mom had made me give her every detail of my breakfast. My answers were like fertilizer; everything I said seemed to generate two or three new questions. Then Mom rehashed through stories about Rick Finzimer: their spring formal, the Broadway play, the picnic out in Valley Forge. This batch of stories must have been true, considering they were so boring and I'd heard them all before.

"Do you still like him or something?" I asked finally. Mom's face had colored and she'd ahemmed a couple of times.

"No, no, no, it's only . . ." But then the phone rang and it was Rick Finzimer with directions to his parents' house and she had talked to him forever in a quiet sweet-as-honey voice. She probably managed to get in some more brags about me during that call, too.

"Ricky played basketball." Mrs. Finzimer nods. She

stares at her son, who also nods.

"Hmm. I never was one for sports," says Mom. "Unless yoga counts."

I glare at Mom again for saying something so spacey, and then I look down at my blue linen lap and try to take myself away from this dark room full of strangeness. I picture myself shooting baskets in the empty Bradshaw gym, when it's late afternoon in spring. The sun pours through the open doors, and all I can hear is the thud of the ball, the squeak of my shoes. I catch my breath as the ball wobbles, wavers, and then shlummphs soundly through the net. My mind takes shot after perfect shot, even after we stand up and move into the dining room for lunch.

"Sit, please." Mrs. Finzimer beams at me and Mom. "And please, start." I sit and immediately take a roast beef sandwich off the platter in the middle of the table. "That's right, just dig in," says Mrs. Finzimer, pulling back a chair across from me. Mom sits next to me and clears her throat, her fingers touching light on my spine. I straighten up and adjust my headband.

As soon as I'm into my second bite of sandwich, I feel Mrs. Finzimer's gaze intent on me. "Well, you're the hungry one. Is this when you normally have lunch?"

she asks. "On days when you do go to school?"

My mouth is full but I feel obliged to give her an answer, so I look to Mom for help.

"Danny's out today because it's a special occasion," Mom says. "It's not every day she gets to meet her grandparents—grandmother, I guess I should say."

"What's taking Dad so long?" Rick Finzimer suddenly jumps out of his chair and strides out of the room, shouting, "Dad! Dad! What are you doing out there? We're starting lunch!"

"Ricky had perfect attendance records three years straight," Mrs. Finzimer says softly, smiling down at her plate. "Third grade to sixth. Not even the flu, not once, until junior high."

Nobody answers her. The back door bangs as Rick Finzimer steps outside. *My grandparents have a squeaky back door.*

As soon as he's gone the smile drops right off Mrs. Finzimer's soft pigeon face. She stares across the table at Mom, her arms stretched out in front of her and her hands balled into one fist, like a mallet dividing the space between them.

"He hasn't told them, Susan," says Mrs. Finzimer.

"I'm sorry?" Mom's politeness smile freezes and holds.

"Ricky hasn't told Caren and Morgan and Madison about you and ah, and ah, Danny. He's not planning on it. Too upsetting, he thinks. And I surely don't blame him. My boy's had a hard enough time just getting himself on his feet, figuring out his own life. Now he's got this baseball cap business going, and another family— his real family, in my honest opinion, and . . . he doesn't need this, you know. He didn't ask for this. None of us asked for this. Taking our name, even. I hope you don't mind my speaking straight."

I wonder what happened to the sweet lady who pledged twenty dollars on her credit card to raise money for her son's alma mater. The woman I am staring at has a closed, judging face that forces us to acknowledge her distaste of us. It's truly a punishment to have to stare back at her. I feel the warm, salty beginning of tears in my nose and eyes. I glance at Mom and for a minute I think she might cry, too. Maybe it's her braided hair or the normal clothes, but she looks more like a younger, shyer version of the regular mom I know. She doesn't cry, though. She looks scared but she smiles, instead, and takes a deep breath. When she speaks, her voice is cold as the sweat that breaks across my forehead, but the sound of it dries up all my thoughts of tears.

"I think maybe you need to get one thing straight here," Mom begins. Her chin is level to the table and she speaks in loud, calm, careful words. "My daughter and I have done more than okay for ourselves for fourteen years." Her face loses its fear and her voice builds slowly, the way it sometimes does onstage, and I feel a kind of shelter in it. "Fourteen years. And no one worries about us except us. That's the way we like it. No matter what our last name happens to be, we're all the family we need. Anything else"— she presses the palms of her hands against the edge of the table and the skin under her eyes tightens for a moment, like a pulse point— "anything else is as unexpected as it is unnecessary."

The room is quiet, until I remember that my mouth is full of roast beef, which I then swallow with a loud *gulunk*.

Mrs. Finzimer takes a baby sip from her water glass and licks her lips several times after she's done.

"Well, good then," she says.

When Rick Finzimer comes back in, Mrs. Finzimer unpacks her crooked-tooth smile and cements it right back on her face like nothing happened. I take another sandwich off the tray, although I can feel my stomach groaning from the weight of too much food.

"Dad's not . . . he isn't . . ." Rick Finzimer makes a limp gesture with his shoulders as he sits back down to the lunch. "He's busy."

"We'll just have to get along without him, huh?" Mom clasps her hands together. Her voice has changed; suddenly it's loud and full of pep and she reminds me of someone. Then I guess who. Mom has melted into an imitation of perky Mrs. Paulson. A pretty fair one, too.

Two can play that game, I decide. Because right now, deciding to be someone else *(finally, in one of the most difficult roles ever given to a child actor . . .)* seems like not a bad idea. I raise my eyebrows and drop my chin, holding myself up straight. I look at my grandmother and try to think of what Antonia de Ver White's eyes would see.

"Tell me more about your cats," I say pleasantly. "They're so beautiful."

"Why, let me think." Mrs. Finzimer settles back with a thoughtful, storytelling look in her eye. "I must have started on my first cat just after Nixon was elected."

After lunch, Rick Finzimer makes another trip out to the woodshed and Mrs. Finzimer retreats to the kitchen to make a pot of decaffeinated tea and dessert. She doesn't let us help her.

"Go on out to the porch, enjoy the early spring," she says, shooing us off with her hands. "I'll be right along."

So Mom and I find ourselves alone on the porch in weather that's just a little bit too cold to be pleasant. We sit on the rocking chairs with only the cats to watch over us, and we rock back and forth in uncertain, wood-creaking silence.

"This is just terrible," I finally whisper.

"The pits," she agrees.

"If I could go back in time I would have looked a lot more carefully at those envelopes." I hold my face in my hands and shake my head. "It's so easy for me to get lost in my own little world and do flaky, distracted things like that."

"We all need our own little worlds, sometimes," Mom says quietly. "I remember I made up this game when you were little, and we were still living in Philadelphia. I'd push you in your stroller and we'd walk in a straight line down Walnut Street, and I'd imagine that every block would unwind a year of my life, and then I'd think back on all the years of mistakes I made. Like the year I ran away from my first foster home, the year I fell in love with Rick, the year I didn't try for that navy scholarship because I could only do four push-ups, which seemed like more of an obstacle at the time.

"Anyway, when I'd undone all those years, then I'd turn around and we'd walk back a new, different way, though Rittenhouse Square or Old City. That's when I'd make up exactly how I would have changed each year, made it work out better for us."

"For you," I correct. "If you undid the year you met *him*, you would undo the year of having me, right?" I glance at her out of the corners of my eyes.

Mom looks even smaller than usual, like she would break if you touched her. Her face is thoughtful and she leans way back in her rocking chair, her hands gripping the sides and she drops her chin back like a little kid, staring way up at the porch eaves. She tips so far back that I have a hand braced to catch her in case she falls over.

"Nope, never," she says finally, and her words aren't big and dramatic, but come out from right inside her thinking. "I never walked those blocks without you in my plan. Never, Danny. You're my family."

Her walking game sort of reminds me of *The Odyssey,* so I tell her about Penelope weaving and unraveling her tapestry, but Mom just gets that happy look on her face when she thinks of me getting my good Bradshaw education.

"That Dr. Sonenshine used to teach at Amherst," she says. "Maybe you'll go there, one day."

"Maybe," I say.

"Speaking of going." Mom squints out to the driveway where Old Yeller is parked behind the Finzimer sedan. "You want to make a break for it?"

"Race you." But she's already jumped up so fast that I just barely save her rocker from tipping and crashing over.

Later, of course, we apologize.

"It was that horseradish on the roast beef," Mom explains over the phone while I sit at the kitchen table, a hand clapped over my mouth. Mom's lies flow so effortlessly, it's actually pretty astounding. "She's deathly allergic, and when she started going into fits on the porch . . . Yes, yes, I tried calling your mother, but she was back in the kitchen. . . . Of course I rushed her right to the hospital just in time. . . . Now? Let me check." Mom looks at me and points to the receiver but I slice my hands through the air and shake my head quickly. If I talked now, I'd start laughing. "She's still feeling a little too weak to talk. . . . Yes, I'll tell her to give you a ring before you leave."

I call later that night, before Rick Finzimer's next morning flight home.

"If you need anything," he says. "You have my work number."

"Okay, thanks."

"And take care. It was nice to meet you, Danny."

"Yep. You, too."

"Next time I'm in town, we could go have lunch or something."

"I'd like that, I think."

He says good-bye, and I hang up and breathe a long sigh. I'm relieved but also a little sad. When Rick Finzimer was just a smiling picture on the bookshelf, he seemed full of secrets and possibilities. Now that the mystery of Rick Finzimer has been solved, my imagination can't control him anymore.

"I don't even know why I care," I explained to Gary. "It's hard to say if he's even worth knowing."

"But that's what you miss—the person you'll never know," Gary said. Which is true. Whenever I miss Elliot, it comes down to specifics, like how he loved to listen to 98.5 Lite Hits, no matter how much Mom and I made fun of him. Or how calm he was when Portia stepped on a bee—Elliot just packed her foot with ice and baking soda and said, "Cry it all out, and the pain'll go away quicker," which is the exact right thing to say to someone who loves to cry as much as Portia.

But I don't have any memories like that of Rick Finzimer. There's an ache inside me where all those memories should be. It's a different feeling from missing Elliot, but it's painful all the same.

The following Sunday morning I slap my alarm off and jump out of bed, into the shower and then a pair of jeans, sneakers, and an old T-shirt. Mom's already gone and I take the train with a fast-beating heart. I hope I know what I'm doing.

Esther is waiting for me in the kitchen.

"It's real simple," she says, tying a black apron around my waist. "Just clear the empty plates, dump ashtrays after two butts, restock the iced-tea stations, and you have to get lemons from the walk-in fridge. You know how to make coffee? Good. And do napkin rolls whenever you can grab a minute. You get ten percent of the wait staff's tips; it's all under the table."

"Okay, got it."

"Your mom's really funny; she recruited me for the play, for *Tom!*—not that I'm any good, but she was always like, 'Esther, you're such a perfect mimic,' so in the end I was like, 'Okay I'll give it a shot.' It's just a small part." Esther squares her shoulders. "But I do kind of like to imitate other people's voices just for fun. It was so weird how your mom just knew . . ." She smiles and picks up a box of Sweet'n Low packets. "Also, every table gets waters as soon as they're seated. And babies get those special seats over by the bar. Good luck."

I spy Mom before she sees me. She's putting an order into the computer and frowning, and a couple of irritated waitresses wait behind her, all rolling eyes and tapping feet. I guess Mom's waitressing skills haven't improved much since Portia saw her in action a few weeks ago.

"Hey." I wave when she looks up. "What a coincidence. This is my new part-time job, too."

When I see the surprise in Mom's face, I'm glad that I know how to make a few good decisions alongside the dumb ones.

CHAPTER

10

THE TOM SAWYER MUSICAL slowly begins taking hold of Mom's life, especially after *As You Like It* wraps up. The play wasn't a big success, and they ended up closing early. Shakespeare is always something of a hit or miss at Bellmont.

As the days count down to opening night, Mom's at Bradshaw all the time, and even when she comes home, she's still absentmindedly wearing parts of the school like a costume: a highlighter pen to hold her hair up in a bun, bracelets of paper clips or rubber bands, a few fingernails painted in with purple Magic Marker or Wite-Out. She seems completely obsessive and a little out of her mind, so I do my best to avoid her when we're both at school.

"It's got to work," she'll occasionally say out of the blue, clenching her fists and staring at me.

"Mom, of course it'll work," I always reply, but to

me *Tom!* sounds like a play that's bogged down with uncertainties.

For one thing, Claire Knoxworthy, the tenth-grader who's playing Tom, is one of the saddest sacks ever to hit Bradshaw. She's a nervous, scurrying, beetle-faced girl whom kids have called "The Pox" since lower school. The name fits her, since she has that sort of medieval plague-struck look to her. Definitely not Tom Sawyer cute, unless you've always pictured Tom with goose white skin and a crooked Dutch Boy haircut.

I don't know too much about Claire except that she has a younger sister who takes the special ed. bus, and both Knoxworthy girls live with just their grandmother. Claire did distinguish herself last year when she tried to found the Young Astronomers club for Wednesday activities. People signed up with names like Ima Starr and Dija Moonme, but poor Claire didn't get it and on Wednesday she even brought punch and vanilla wafers to school, because she thought she'd have such a big turnout. I heard the whole story when I was in the infirmary, faking a headache, and so the only way I can ever think about Claire is with RTs.

"She'll be great," Mom says. "She has pizzazz, and her voice is unbeatable."

"Even if she is great," I told Portia, "most people will have a hard time forgetting that it's Claire. Claire's just so . . . Claire."

"We'll just clap extra hard," Portia said. "My parents'll be there, and Mom's a professional at getting a crowd going."

Another problem is Ms. Kohlman, who plays the piano.

"We have issues," Mom confesses. I got to see one of these issues unfold when I stood in on an early rehearsal. It was during the Huck and Becky duet.

"Huck and Becky!" Ms. Kohlman had suddenly shouted. "Move downstage now!" She'd stopped playing the piano, catching Huck and Becky midnote.

"Too awkward," Mom said, fluttering her fingers dismissively.

"I'm not sure." Ms. Kohlman stood, waddled on her stumpy walrus legs over to where Mom sat, and pointed up to the stage. "They're losing the whole back of the house."

"Not at all." Mom stood up, too. "You're a hundred percent wrong."

"I think you're being a little bit of a diva, Sue," Ms. Kohlman shot back.

"Who's the director here?" asked Mom.

"If you can't appreciate other people's creative input, maybe you need a new music director," snipped Ms. Kohlman.

"Bea Kohlman better back off," Mom fumed later. "Too many cooks, you know."

After that episode, the rehearsals made me too nervous to watch. I heard that Ms. Kohlman and Mom's regular sparring matches have been a source of endless delight for the whole cast, but I doubt the fighting has done much to help the play.

Meanwhile, after my trial day, I got a regular position at the Greenhouse, busing tables for Sunday brunch. The money helps buy my train pass, but Mom makes me keep the rest for an allowance. Being tall and strong is an asset, and it makes me feel good when I can do something Mom can't, like carry a tray or reach some glasses for her.

One Sunday I lived out a pretty big nightmare when all the Finns came flouncing in for brunch. Of course, Lacy pretended like she had no idea Mom and I worked there.

"Oh wow, that's so funny," she said. "Both of you guys. Good mother-daughter bonding experience."

"Better than mother-daughter liposuction," I returned, but only in my head. Out loud I said, "It's okay."

And it is okay, sort of. Some days I do feel that life has not been overgenerous handing out breaks to Mom and me, and I wish I could benefit from some of the stuff Portia's got, like a beautiful house and perfect hair and a cool dad. But other days I think that working for my own money at the Greenhouse is more mature than getting handouts. As Gary says, it'll get me ready for the real world, which isn't quite as kind or generous as most Saint Germaine parents.

When I'm feeling reasonable, I see it this way. But there are plenty of days I'd trade being mature for great hair.

The afternoon following dress rehearsal, Mom comes home hissing mad.

"Dwight Lemmon is trying to get me fired!" she storms. "I knew it. Listen to this. He had the stage waxed. It's got some kind of high-powered, high-resistance polish. You can see your own reflection in it. We should perform on ice skates. Lemmon says he'd scheduled to have it waxed months ago. I'm so angry. This could be it, Danny. Girls will be breaking their legs, literally. My bags might be packed."

"But you know how to ice-skate, remember?"

"This is not funny, Danny." Mom presses her fingers against her temples.

"What are you going to do?"

"Get down on my hands and knees tomorrow morning and scrub it off, if I have to." Mom's hands are in fists. "This is so typical." She looks pale, and all week tired shadows have darkened the skin just beneath her eyes.

"Wax comes off," I tell her. "And Portia and I'll help scrub." But Mom doesn't hear me; her thoughts are leaping and twirling toward other potential disasters.

That night, I dream about the musical. In my dream, the whole cast of girls is running out of the wings, all these dancing bodies moving simultaneously, and they're slipping and wobbling and starting to fall. I'm hunched in the audience, close to the burning footlights and holding a sack full of rock salt, which I'm throwing by handfuls onto the stage, so that it scatters over the waxed surface like diamonds. "It's okay," I'm mouthing to Mom, who stands in the wings. "It's only rock salt, rock salt." But she can't hear me. Her face, half hidden by the long folds of the curtain, looks gray and frightened.

Right in that blip of time before I'm fully awake, I'm happily thinking how rock salt is a brilliant idea that will save the show. Then I wake all the way up and feel like an idiot.

I tell Mom my dream on the way to school the next morning.

"Dreams," she sniffs. "They're so useless in real life. Whenever they happen in a book or a movie and they're supposed to be all symbolic and problem solving, I always want to scream fake, fake, fake. If I ever was a movie director or something, dreams would be the first things I'd permanently veto."

"The worst is how I thought I'd solved it," I say, sipping carefully from my coffee. Ever since he came back from the shop, Old Yeller's gear has been sticking when Mom shifts into third.

"Well, late last night I lay awake for hours and I think I did solve it," she says. She pauses. "Sawdust," she pronounces. "I'm going to put an inch of it down everywhere. It'll be cute; it'll look like the outdoors."

Sawdust. I'm not sure. To me, this idea seems kind of messy.

Later that day, Mom brushes past me on the stairs and she doesn't even see me. Her gaze is fixed in the distance as if to anchor the thoughts racing inside her head and she's carrying a stack of programs, too many for one person. A few flap out and drop like wounded birds on the stairs behind her.

After lunch, I catch sight of Mr. Lemmon in the faculty lounge, sipping his tea and reading a magazine. His legs are crossed at the ankle and his whole body seems content and well rested. When he sees me he prisses up his face in a smile.

He's planning to fire her, I think. My mind is already jumping ahead to figure out if I could pick up alternate Thursday nights and Saturday lunches at the Greenhouse. Foxwood High isn't so bad, I tell myself. It's just a fear of the unknown, combined with a slight anxiety about the metal detectors outside the front doors that check students for firearms.

Ty Amblin is the first person I see when Gary and Portia and I walk into the front lobby on opening night. For once, Portia says and does everything exactly right.

"I see him," she whispers, not looking at him. "So just keep talking to me and we'll go over to the refreshment table for food and then head through the farthest left-hand doors."

"Don't look at him," I say.

"No way. Smile. You look insecure."

Even as Portia and Gary and I file into our seats, my eyes are trained on Ty. He pretends not to notice me, either, but right until the moment the house lights fall, I observe the outline of his shiny yellow hair and wonder if I'll ever get over all my weird like and hate feelings for him, and if I'll ever really know why he ditched before the Fling. "Who cares?" I mumble to myself under my breath. "You do," answers the mean little voice deep inside me who always likes to cut and scrape me with the truth.

When the act 1 curtain comes up and a single spotlight beams down on Claire Knoxworthy, who's wearing a straw hat and an extraspooked expression, a ripple of laughter washes the air. I scrunch down in my seat and Portia grips my knee.

"Clap no matter what," I whisper. Portia nods.

It's the last worry I have all night. Because *Tom!* turns out to be a play that explodes in front of everyone's eyes like bright hot firecrackers. It's a play I never could have envisioned myself; the effect reminds me of the quick, timed teamwork in a perfect basketball game, and finally I understand what Mom was talking about with all her wild gestures and explanations about space and athletes and movement.

There were a thousand perfect moments: Gray Fitzpatrick, as Becky, doing a send-up of her own boy-crazy self. And Esther's accent. And Tonya Beirhorst's double backflip. And Mom's decision to use broomsticks as banjos in one ensemble number that had the audience laughing so hard it drowned out the singing chorus.

But I think my favorite moment was seeing Claire Knoxworthy's face after her first solo. She deserved it, of course. She was probably the most talented person ever to step onto that stage since it had been built, and she deserved every second and decibel of that storm of applause that likely could have been heard from the parking lot. But Claire's scared, proud little face—visible for just a second underneath Tom's confident, cheery one—when people actually stood up and cheered: I'll never forget it. It's a story I can tell people one day when I see her name light up Broadway.

Another great expression of the night belonged to Mr. Lemmon, when I saw him in the lobby at intermission. I was enjoying his undisguised shock so much I didn't even notice Ty Amblin until he was standing right beside me, biting into a macadamia nut cookie. He must not have realized I was standing beside him either, because when he met my gaze he looked startled.

"Danny, hi." One arm quickly swipes the crumbs from his upper lip. "You're not in your uniform." His eyes shift from my dress, my yellow Nyheim dress I would have worn to the Fling. He then checks his gaze over to his parents, who are standing by the front door talking to the Wilders. I can tell he wants to join them.

"I wear other stuff besides uniforms."

"Sure, it's just that . . . so the play's pretty good, huh? Not like that yawn—was it *Saint Joan?*—last year."

"My mom directed this one."

"No kidding. Cool. She had the right idea, making Hannah play that Aunt Polly. Hannah's so bossy."

"She boss you around?" I ask. I wish I had a prop, a soda can or a cookie of my own. Something to make my arms not feel so long and floppy. I cross my arms in front of my chest, even though Portia says you should never do that when speaking to a guy, since it makes you look unapproachable and defensive. Sure enough, Ty takes a half step back from me.

"Ever since we were little kids. But I didn't realize that you guys weren't that good of friends."

"What do you mean? We get along okay."

Ty looks down and rubs a gold button on his sports

jacket. "Oh, I don't know. She just told me some stuff about how you guys didn't really click."

Hannah. She probably told him I wasn't good enough to go to the dance with. Probably made up stuff, told him I'd wear something ugly, those zip boots maybe. It makes me furious, thinking of them talking about me like that, and not knowing exactly what they said. Just ask him, I think. Just do it.

I think of Mom facing off against Mrs. Finzimer, the way she spoke so strong and clear, her voice hard as a brick wall against the little poison arrows of Mrs. Finzimer's contempt. I open my mouth.

"Ty, I hope you don't mind me speaking straight." My voice is more polite than Mom's and a little more wobbly. I can't make myself look straight into his eyes so I stare at his hand holding the cookie. His fingernails are just as clean and polished as always.

"Yeah?"

"Here's the thing. What I was wondering was, if you really did have a family thing that Saturday, or did you just not want to go with me? Because if you didn't—" I stop; Ty is practically backing into the refreshment table, trying to get away from me. I press my lips together. "It's no big deal." I shrug. "You can tell me."

"You're nuts," he says lamely, his voice just breaking into the edge of a whine. "I told you it was my aunt—"

"Okay. I just wanted to know," I say again. I remember what Mr. Paulson said about Ty's being worthy of me. I look straight at Ty. The Smile has been dislodged in place of a worried, wimpy grin. I keep staring, waiting for him to turn and walk away from me. Which he does.

It's not until I get back to my seat that I realize my hands are shaking.

"Saw you guys talking out there. You looked really defensive. What did he say to you?" Portia whispers from behind her program.

"Nothing," I whisper back. "He's got nothing to say. He's not worth talking about."

The second act temporarily dissolves my bad mood, and when the final curtain falls, we're all on our feet. Everyone gets a standing ovation, even the extras. It's like the whole audience has turned into a crowd of Mrs. Paulsons. Then the cast makes Mom come up on the stage and they load her down with huge bouquets of flowers. Mom is in true form, waving and smiling and hopping around, kissing the girls on the tops of their heads. A few kids turn around in their seats to wave at me and give me thumbs-up signs, to show they know how proud I must be of her. I am.

After the play, with a face stiff as Gary's extrastarched dress-up shirt, Mr. Lemmon shakes Mom's hand and congratulates her a few times.

"But didn't it look like he wanted to spit on me?" Mom cackles gleefully as we're walking out to the parking lot afterward.

"He looked totally floored!" I laugh. "He looked like someone had been punching him in the stomach repeatedly, all night long. But Mom, where are we going to put these flowers?" My arms are heavy with the bouquets.

"The back seat's too full. Stick the rest in the trunk."

I pop the trunk to find it full of three enormous bags, lying in a row like a bed full of sleeping children.

"Are you a nut? There must be over fifty pounds of rock salt in here."

"Oh, that's right! I forgot, I bought it today." She puts her fingers over her lips and smiles down sheepishly at the bags. "Your dream. I figured, maybe, if the sawdust didn't work out, and we're lucky it did . . . but, anyway." She gathers a bunch of flowers from me and starts packing them over the salt. "I'd have done anything to save the show," she says.

"You really think rock salt would have worked?" I am incredulous.

"Maybe it's one of those things about being in a family of two." Mom slams the trunk shut and rubs her hands together briskly to clean them. "But I put a lot of value on what you say, Danny. Even the off-the-wall stuff that comes to you in dreams. And sometimes those outrageous solutions work better than the obvious ones."

"Like Claire Knoxworthy."

"Yep, just like Claire. And to me, that's the greatest thing about theater," Mom says. "Its doors are open widest to the Claire Knoxworthys of the world. People who don't belong anywhere always belong on a stage."

Later that spring, Bradshaw offers Mom a full-time job as school arts coordinator, which she accepts. She'll be working in all the classes, from the kindergarten to the twelfth grade, helping them put together their plays and recitals. Basically, it's a job the school tailored to fit Mom's talents. Since the money that *Tom!* brings in actually nets a profit instead of a loss for the first time in Bradshaw history, the school decides it would be a lucrative idea to keep Mom working there.

She quits the Greenhouse the same day she signs the Bradshaw contract, and the first thing she does to celebrate is to book a mother-daughter dentist trip—four pulled wisdom teeth for her and four fillings for me, under our new insurance coverage.

I stay on at the Greenhouse, though, working the Sunday brunch shift. It's good money, and I need to start saving for my own car. Old Yeller is not ever going to be a coolmobile.

But we don't know any of that as we're driving home, not that we need any cheering up. We stop at the 7-Eleven for root beer and vanilla ice cream, and we stay up late that night, sitting on the couch and talking about the play. I also finally spill out the whole entire Ty Amblin story to her, even though my chest blotches up the whole time I'm talking.

"Ty Amblin doesn't seem to offer much more than a good haircut." Mom points her ice-cream spoon at me. "He would bore you, Danny. He was a sweet boy, but he grew up to be a bland-o. A Celia."

"A Rick Finzimer," I add, which makes her laugh.

"You're right. So don't marry him. I mean, don't marry him, but don't do what I did, except I mean that I don't regret—"

"I know what you mean, Mom." I reach over and pat her knee.

The cream-colored business envelope arrives in our mailbox few days later. It's neatly typed to Antonia de Ver White and stamped with first-class postage. I drop my barn jacket and book bag in a heap on the floor; already my face is tensed into a frown of preparation.

Dear Ms. de Ver White:
We are pleased to inform you that your submission, which we are tentatively titling "Dear Rick Finzimer (Dad):" has just won second place in *The Lilac* first page contest. The judges here all agreed that the poignant theme of the writing and your decision to use a letter format really breathed life into the fiction. It seems as though there's quite a story there!
Please call our offices during business hours so that we can take your social security number in order to process your check for $500.00. The story will appear in the May issue of *The Lilac*.

Sincerely,
The Editors

For a crazy minute I think about calling California, just to shout in Rick Finzimer's ear, just to holler, "I won! I won!" and hang up. But the thought burns itself out fast. It would take two seconds to tell him that I won, but it would take forever to explain why the winning matters so much to me. And I don't have that kind of time. Anyway, it's not Rick Finzimer's reaction that I particularly care about.

Before I go to bed, I put the letter in the refrigerator, taped to an empty milk carton, so that Mom will be sure to see it when she gets home from her *Lost in Yonkers* audition. I keep having to stick my head in the refrigerator, though, just to believe the whole thing's for real.

The letter gets me thinking about Dr. Sonenshine and all her endless red-inked comments—all that advice about writing stuff that's true to life. Mostly, though, I think about how five hundred dollars is more money than I ever guessed my life had in store for me right now. It's a glamorous amount of money. I already feel my cheekbones poking out a little.

"That's terrific, Antonia," Gary says when he stops by with a big bowl of spinach salad he supposedly couldn't finish, and I make him look in the fridge. Now he holds me by the nose, using it as a handle to shake my head back and forth. "You're my hero."

"You're *my* hero," I tell him. "What would I have done without my amazing computer setup?"

Gary flushes. "The computer?—that's nothing," he says.

"It's more than just about computers," I insist. "I couldn't ask for anyone better as a friend and a fallback person." I know he doesn't know what I mean exactly, but he looks so proud and flustered, I bet even his frizzy hair would turn pink if it could.

I still think that when I get to college, I'll legally change my name to Antonia de Ver White, but lately Danny Finzimer is turning out to be someone I might not mind being. At least I have a few years to think about it. I go to bed with a smile, ready to wake up at the soft jingle of Mom's keys.